Agatha Christie

The Murder at the Vicarage

Collins

Collins

HarperCollins Publishers
The News Building
1 London Bridge Street
London SE1 9GF

www.collinselt.com

This *Collins English Readers* edition first published by HarperCollins Publishers 2012. This second edition published 2017.

10 9 8 7 6 5 4 3 2 1

First published in Great Britain by Collins 1930

www.agathachristie.com

ISBN: 978-0-00-826231-0

A catalogue record for this book is available from the British Library.

Cover design © HarperCollins*Publishers* Ltd/Agatha Christie Ltd 2017

Typeset by Davidson Publishing Solutions, Glasgow

Printed and bound by CPI Group (UK) Ltd., Croydon, CR0 4YY

Contents

◆ Introduction ◆

About Collins English Readers

Collins English Readers have been created for readers worldwide whose first language is not English. The stories are carefully graded to ensure that you, the reader, will both enjoy and benefit from your reading experience.

Words which are above the required reading level are underlined the first time they appear in a story. All underlined words are defined in the **Glossary** at the back of the book. Books at levels 1 and 2 take their definitions from the *Collins COBUILD Essential English Dictionary*, and books at levels 3 and above from the *Collins COBUILD Advanced English Dictionary*. Where appropriate, definitions are simplified for level and context.

Alongside the glossary, a **Character list** is provided to help the reader identify who is who, and how they are connected to each other. **Cultural notes** explain historical, cultural and other references. **Maps and diagrams** are provided where appropriate. A **downloadable recording** is also available of the full story. To access the audio, go to www.collinselt.com/eltreadersaudio. The password is the fifth word on page 2 of this book.

To support both teachers and learners, additional materials are available online at www.collinselt.com/readers. These include a **Plot synopsis** and **classroom activities** (both for teachers), **Student activities**, a **level checker** and much more.

About Agatha Christie

Agatha Christie

Agatha Christie (1890–1976) is known throughout the world as the Queen of Crime. She is the most widely published and translated author of all time and in any language; only the Bible and Shakespeare have sold more copies.

Agatha Christie's first novel was published in 1920. It featured Hercule Poirot, the Belgian detective who has become the most popular detective in crime fiction since Sherlock Holmes.

Collins has published Agatha Christie since 1926.

The Grading Scheme

The Collins COBUILD Grading Scheme has been created using the most up-to-date language usage information available today. Each level is guided by a comprehensive grammar and vocabulary framework, ensuring that the series will perfectly match readers' abilities.

		CEF band	Pages	Word count	Headwords
Level 1	elementary	A2	64	5,000–8,000	approx. 700
Level 2	pre-intermediate	A2–B1	80	8,000–11,000	approx. 900
Level 3	intermediate	B1	96	11,000–20,000	approx. 1,300
Level 4	upper-intermediate	B2	112-128	15,000–26,000	approx. 1,700
Level 5	upper-intermediate+	B2+	128+	22,000–30,000	approx. 2,200
Level 6	advanced	C1	144+	28,000+	2,500+
Level 7	advanced+	C2	160+	*varied*	*varied*

For more information on the Collins COBUILD Grading Scheme go to www.collinselt.com/readers/gradingscheme.

CHAPTER I

It is difficult to know where to begin this story, but I have chosen a particular Wednesday at the <u>vicarage</u>[1]. This is because the conversation around the table contained details which affected later developments.

I had just finished cutting some meat, which was very tough, and said, waving the knife in a way that was not at all appropriate for a <u>vicar</u>[1], that anyone who murdered <u>Colonel</u> Protheroe would be doing the world a favour.

My young nephew, Dennis, said, 'We'll all remember that when the old man is found covered in blood. And Mary will describe how you waved the knife in a violent manner, won't you, Mary?'

But Mary, who is a servant at the vicarage, just put a dish of unpleasant-looking cabbage on the table and left the room.

'I am sorry that I am so useless at taking care of the house,' said my wife, whose name is Griselda. She is twenty years younger than I am, very pretty, and unable to take anything seriously.

'My dear,' I said, 'if you would only try...'

'But when I'm trying things just get worse. So it is better to leave things to Mary, who gives us awful things to eat. Now, tell me more about Colonel Protheroe.'

'Unpleasant man,' said Dennis. 'It is not surprising that his first wife left him.'

'Darling,' said Griselda, 'Why were you so angry with Colonel Protheroe? Was it anything to do with Mr Hawes?'

Hawes is our new <u>curate</u>[1], whom Colonel Protheroe dislikes.

'No, it was because of Mrs Price Ridley's pound note.'

Mrs Price Ridley, a member of my church, had put a pound note in the <u>collection bag</u>. Later, when she was reading the amount collected on the church notice-board, she saw that no pound note had been received. So she complained to Colonel Protheroe, who is a <u>churchwarden</u>.

'He wants to look at all the church accounts,' I said. 'He's coming here tomorrow evening so we can do it together. Does he think I have stolen church money? But now I must get on with preparing my <u>sermon</u>. What are you doing this afternoon, Griselda?'

'My duty as the wife of a vicar. Tea and talk at four-thirty.'

'Who is coming?'

'Mrs Price Ridley, Miss Wetherby, Miss Hartnell, and that terrible Miss Marple.'

'I rather like Miss Marple,' I said. 'She has a sense of humour.'

'And she always knows every single thing that happens in the village,' said Griselda. 'And explains them in the worst possible way.'

'Well, don't expect me in for tea,' said Dennis. 'The Protheroes have invited me to play tennis today. What luck.' He quickly left the room and Griselda and I went into my study.

'I wonder what we will talk about at tea,' said Griselda. 'Mrs Lestrange, I suppose. It's so mysterious, isn't it, the way she suddenly rented a house here, and hardly ever goes outside it? It's like a detective story. You know – "Who is she, the mysterious woman with the pale, beautiful face? Nobody knows."'

'You read too many detective stories,' I said. 'Now, I must start my sermon.'

'Do you know,' said Griselda, 'I could have married a politician, a <u>lord</u>, a rich businessman, but instead I chose you? Didn't that surprise you?'

'Yes. I've often wondered why.'

Griselda laughed. 'It made me feel powerful. The other men all thought I was wonderful. But I am the sort of woman you most dislike, and yet you <u>adore</u> me, don't you?'

'I do care about you, my dear.'

'Oh! Len, you adore me,' Griselda said. 'But you don't deserve me. So I will have a love affair with the artist who is painting my picture. I will. Just think of the talk in the village.' She kissed me, and stepped through the open glass door into the garden.

Chapter 2

I had been in a good mood for writing, but now I felt uncomfortable. Then, as I picked up my pen, Lettice Protheroe wandered in.

Lettice is a pretty girl, tall and fair and delicate. She came through the glass door, pulled off her little yellow hat and said, 'Is Dennis about?'

There is a path from Old Hall[2], where she lives, to our garden gate, so most people coming from there come to the study window instead of going along the road to the front door.

'Dennis said he was going to play tennis at your place. He said you had asked him.'

Lettice sat down on the sofa. 'I think I did. Only that was Friday. And today is Tuesday.'

'It's Wednesday,' I said.

'Oh. Then is Griselda here?'

'She's in the studio with Lawrence Redding.'

'There's been some trouble about him,' said Lettice. 'With father.'

'What about?' I asked.

'About him painting my picture. I was wearing my <u>bathing dress.</u> Father found out about it. It really is stupid – I go on the beach in my bathing dress, but now father won't allow Lawrence into the house. If I had some money, I would go away. If father died, then I would be all right.'

'You must not say things like that, Lettice.'

'Well, I'm not surprised my mother left him. Do you know, for years I believed she was dead. I wonder where she is. Father's new wife, Anne, hates me.' She got up. 'I must go. I said I would look at Dr Stone's <u>barrow</u>[3].' And she wandered out again, and across the garden.

I thought about Dr Stone, who was a well-known <u>archaeologist</u>. He had come to stay at the Blue Boar <u>Inn</u>, while he examined an old <u>burial ground</u> on Colonel Protheroe's land. There had already been a disagreement between them.

I wondered how Lettice would get on with Dr Stone's secretary. Miss Cram is a healthy young woman, with pink cheeks and a loud voice. She is the complete opposite of Lettice.

I had one more interruption. My curate, Hawes, wanted to know if my interview with Protheroe had anything to do with him. I told him that it had not.

Then I saw that the hands of the clock pointed to a quarter to five, which meant that it was really half past four, so I got up and went to the sitting room. Four ladies, holding teacups, were gathered there with Griselda. I sat down between Miss Marple and Miss Wetherby.

'We were just talking', said Griselda, 'about Dr Stone and Miss Cram.'

'No nice girl would do it,' Miss Wetherby said.

'Do what?' I asked.

'Be a secretary to an unmarried man.'

'Oh, my dear,' said Miss Marple. 'I think married ones are the worst.'

'Don't you think,' said my wife, 'that Miss Cram might just like having an interesting job?'

There was silence. Then Miss Marple touched Griselda's arm. 'You think the best of everyone.'

'But do you really think she is attracted to that boring old man?' Griselda said.

'He got angry with Colonel Protheroe the other day,' said Miss Marple. 'The Colonel accused him of knowing nothing about archaeology.'

'How like Colonel Protheroe, and what nonsense,' said Mrs Price Ridley.

'Very like Colonel Protheroe, but perhaps it was not nonsense,' said Miss Marple. 'We do sometimes trust people too easily.'

'There has also been some talk about that young artist, Mr Redding, hasn't there?' said Miss Wetherby.

'Did Lettice tell you about it?' Miss Marple asked me. 'I saw her go round to the study window.' Miss Marple lives next door and sees everything, usually when she is gardening.

'She mentioned it, yes,' I admitted.

'Oh!' cried Miss Wetherby. 'And I saw Dr Haydock coming out of Mrs Lestrange's cottage.'

'Perhaps she's ill,' suggested Mrs Price Ridley.

'No,' said Miss Hartnell. 'I saw her walking round her garden this afternoon.'

'She and Dr Haydock may be old friends,' said Mrs Price Ridley.

'Yes. I do know...' said Griselda.

Everyone leaned forward.

'...that when they were abroad, her husband was killed. And Dr Haydock rescued her.'

The excitement rose, then Miss Marple said, 'Bad girl! If you make things up, people often believe them, and sometimes that leads to problems.'

'I wonder if there is a romance between the artist Lawrence Redding and Lettice Protheroe,' said Miss Wetherby.

'Not Lettice.' Miss Marple seemed thoughtful. 'But perhaps another person.'

She was looking at Griselda as she spoke, and I suddenly felt very angry. 'Don't you think, Miss Marple,' I said, 'that problems may be caused by careless talk?'

'Dear Vicar,' said Miss Marple, 'careless talk is often unkind, but it is also often true.'

'Awful old woman,' said Griselda, when the ladies had gone. 'Len, do you really think I am having a romance with Lawrence Redding?'

'No, of course not. But I do wish you would be more careful in what you say.'

'Lawrence never even tries to kiss to me,' she said. 'I can't understand why.'

'He knows that you're a married woman. You don't want him to kiss you, do you?'

'Not really,' said Griselda. 'If he's in love with Lettice Protheroe...'

'Miss Marple didn't think he was.'

'Miss Marple may be wrong.'

'She never is.'

Griselda paused, then said, 'You do believe me, don't you? When I say there's nothing between Lawrence and me.'

'My dear,' I said. 'Of course.'

'Dear Len.' My wife kissed me. 'You'd believe me whatever I said, wouldn't you?' And then she left the room.

There were very few people that evening at the Wednesday church service, but afterwards, as I left, I saw a woman standing and looking up at one of our coloured-glass windows. It was Mrs Lestrange.

'These windows are beautiful,' she said.

We walked down the road which went past her house. When we reached her gate, she said, 'Please, come in and tell me what you think of my new home.'

It was arranged very simply, but perfectly, and I wondered what had made Mrs Lestrange come to St Mary Mead. It seemed odd for such a cultured woman to be living in a small country village.

She was a very tall woman. Her hair was red gold and her make-up was perfect. She also had the most unusual eyes I have ever seen – for they were almost golden, too. While we talked about pictures, books and old churches, I felt that Mrs Lestrange really wanted to talk to me about something else. When I left to go home, I looked back and saw her watching me with an anxious expression.

'If there is anything I can do…' I said.

'It's very kind of you,' she replied. 'It's difficult. No, I don't think anyone can help me.'

I returned to the vicarage by the garden gate. As I closed it, I suddenly decided to go down to our shed, which Lawrence Redding was using as a studio, to look at Griselda's picture while no one was there. I opened the door and then stopped. There was a man and a woman in the studio. The man's arms were round the woman and he was kissing her.

The two people were Lawrence Redding, and Mrs Protheroe.

I backed out and walked quickly to my study. The discovery was a great shock to me. Suddenly there was a knock on the glass door. I got up to open it and Mrs Protheroe came straight in. The quiet, controlled, woman had disappeared. Instead I was looking at a quick-breathing, desperate creature. For the first time, I realized that Anne Protheroe was beautiful. She had brown hair, a pale face and very deep grey eyes. 'You – you saw just now?' she said.

'Yes.'

'We love each other…'

I said nothing.

'I suppose to you that is very wrong?'

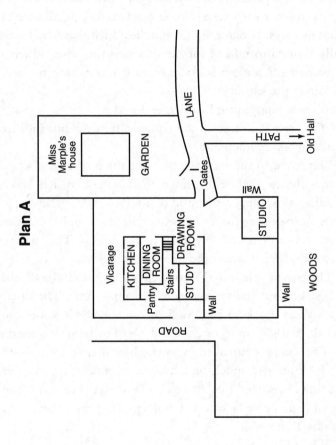

Plan A

'You are a married woman…'

'Oh! Do you think I haven't thought about that again and again? I'm not a bad woman. I just don't know what to do. I'm so unhappy. No woman could be happy with my husband. I wish he was dead. That's awful, but I do…'

I said the things to her that it was my duty to say, remembering all the time how that morning I had said that a world without Colonel Protheroe would be a better place.

When she left, she thanked me. But I felt worried because I now knew that Anne Protheroe was the kind of woman who would stop at nothing when her emotions took control. And she was madly in love with Lawrence Redding.

CHAPTER 4

I had completely forgotten that we had asked Lawrence Redding to dinner that night. When Griselda told me, I was shocked.

'I've thought about what you said at lunch,' she told me, 'and I've found some good things to eat.'

Sadly our dinner only proved Griselda had been right when she'd said that the more she tried, the worse things went. The menu was expensive, but Mary seemed to have enjoyed undercooking and overcooking everything. However, Lawrence Redding was a very good guest. He has dark hair, his eyes are bright blue, and he can tell a good story. Griselda and Dennis kept telling jokes and Lawrence cheerfully joined in. However, I was not surprised when after dinner he suggested we went to my study.

As soon as we were alone his manner changed. 'This isn't the usual sort of love affair between Anne and me.'

I told him that people had been saying that since the beginning of time, and a strange little smile touched his lips. 'Of course, if this were a book, the old man would die – and no one would be sorry.'

I told him that was a cruel thing to say.

'Oh! I didn't mean I was going to put a knife in his back, though I'd thank anyone who did. I'm surprised the first Mrs Protheroe didn't kill him. You don't know how Anne suffers. If I had enough money, I'd take her away now.'

Then I spoke to him very seriously and asked him to leave St Mary Mead. If he stayed, people would start to talk about his relationship with Anne. Colonel Protheroe would hear about it – and things would be made much worse for her.

'But everyone thinks my interest is in Lettice.'

'Haven't you thought,' I asked, 'that Lettice might think that, too?'

Lawrence seemed surprised. Lettice didn't care about him at all. At that moment Griselda and Dennis came in and said I must not stop Lawrence from enjoying himself.

'Oh, how I would like some excitement,' Griselda said. 'A murder – or just a robbery.'

'I don't suppose there's anything worth stealing,' said Lawrence. 'Unless we stole Miss Hartnell's false teeth.'

'They do make an awful noise,' said Griselda. 'But you're wrong about there being nothing worth stealing. There's some wonderful old silver at Old Hall, including a seventeenth century *tazza*. Worth thousands of pounds.'

'The old man would probably shoot you,' said Dennis.

'Oh, we'd get in first and tell him to put his hands up!' said Griselda. 'Has anyone got a gun?'

'I've got a <u>Mauser</u>,' said Lawrence.

'How exciting. Why do you have it?'

'Souvenir of the war.'

'Protheroe was showing the silver to Dr Stone today,' said Dennis. 'Stone was pretending to be very interested in it.'

'Well,' Lawrence said, 'I must go. Thank you for a very pleasant evening.'

On Thursday I was leaving the church and going home for lunch when I met Colonel Protheroe.

'That criminal Mr Archer,' he shouted. 'He came out of prison yesterday and is promising to punish me! Why? Because when I, as a <u>magistrate,</u> sent him to prison I did not consider his wife and children. What nonsense. I am sure you agree with me.'

'You forget,' I said. 'As a vicar I believe in <u>forgiveness</u>.'

'Nonsense! What we need is strong Christianity. So, I'll come to the vicarage this evening, as we arranged, at a quarter past six.' And he walked away.

I went home, had lunch, and went out again to visit some people. Griselda had gone to London by the cheap Thursday train. When I returned at about a quarter to four Mary told me that Mr Redding was waiting for me in the study.

He looked very pale. 'Vicar, you were right. I must leave the village.'

'I think you have made the right decision,' I said.

'Will you look after Anne?'

'Of course. I will do everything I can to help her.'

'Thank you.' He shook my hand. 'I will leave tomorrow.'

When he had gone, I tried to write my sermon, but at half-past five the telephone rang. I was told that Mr Abbott of Low Farm was dying and asked to come at once.

Low Farm was nearly two miles away and I could not possibly get back by six-fifteen. I rang up Old Hall, but I was informed that Colonel Protheroe had just gone out. So I told Mary that I would try to be back by six-thirty, and left.

CHAPTER 5

It was nearly seven when I returned. As I reached the vicarage gate it opened and Lawrence Redding came out. He was shaking all over.

'Hello,' I said. 'Sorry I was out. Come back. I've got to see Protheroe, but we won't be long.'

'Protheroe.' He began to laugh. 'Oh, you'll see Protheroe all right! Oh, yes!'

Worried, I stretched out a hand towards him.

'No,' he shouted. 'I've got to get away. I've got to think.' And he began to run down the road.

I went on into the vicarage. The front door is always open, but I rang the bell and Mary answered it.

'Is Colonel Protheroe here?' I asked her.

'He has been here since a quarter past six.'

'And Mr Redding has been here?'

'He came a few minutes ago. I told him you would be back soon and that Colonel Protheroe was waiting in the study. He said he'd wait too. He's in there now.'

'No, he isn't,' I said. 'I've just met him outside.'

'Well, he can't have stayed more than two minutes.'

I went down the passage and opened the study door. I took a few steps across the room and then stopped. I couldn't understand what was in front of me.

Colonel Protheroe was lying across my desk. There was a pool of some dark liquid by his head, and it was <u>dripping</u> on to the floor. I went across to him. His skin was cold. The man was dead – shot through the head.

I called Mary and I ordered her to run and fetch Dr Haydock. Haydock is a big man with an honest face. When he arrived, he bent over Colonel Protheroe and examined him, then he looked at me. 'He's dead – he's been dead for half an hour, I think.'

'Suicide?'

'No. Look at the position of the wound. And where's the weapon? I'd better call the police.' He picked up the telephone and gave the facts as simply as possible.

'Is it murder?' I asked.

'Looks like it.'

'There's one rather strange thing,' I said. 'This afternoon I was asked to go to a dying man, but when I got there everyone was very surprised. The man was much better, and his wife said she had not telephoned me.'

'So, someone wanted to get you out of the vicarage,' Haydock said. 'Where's your wife?'

'Gone up to London for the day.'

'And the servant?'

'In the kitchen – at the other side of the house.'

'Where she wouldn't hear anything that went on in the study. Who knew that Protheroe was coming here this evening?'

'He mentioned it this morning in the village, very loudly as usual.'

'So everyone knew!'

There was the sound of feet in the passage outside, then the door opened.

'Good evening, gentlemen, I'm Constable Hurst. The Inspector[4] will be here soon. Until then I will ask the questions.' He took out his notebook.

I repeated my story of discovering the body. Then he turned to the doctor. 'In your opinion, Dr Haydock, what was the cause of death?'

'Shot through the head.'

'And the weapon?'

'I can't be sure until we get the bullet out. But it was probably a small <u>pistol</u> – say a Mauser .25.'

I suddenly remembered the conversation last night, and Lawrence Redding telling us he had a Mauser.

Hurst asked Dr Haydock, 'When, in your opinion, did the death happen?'

'He has been dead just over half an hour, I think. Certainly not longer.'

At this moment Inspector Slack arrived. I've never met a man more different from his name. He was not just very energetic, but also extremely rude and bossy. Inspector Slack took his constable's notebook, read it, and <u>strode</u> over to the body. Then he looked at the things on the desk and examined the blood. 'Ah!' he said. 'When he fell forward, the clock was pushed over and it stopped. That will give us the time of the crime. Twenty-two minutes past six. What time did you say he died, doctor?'

'I said about half an hour, but...'

The Inspector looked at his watch. 'Five minutes past seven. I heard about it ten minutes ago, at five to seven. Discovery of the body was at about a quarter to seven. And if you examined it at ten minutes to... Why, that brings it to the same second almost!'

I had been trying to speak. 'About the clock...'

'Sir, I'll ask you any questions I want to know. Time is short. What I want is silence.'

'Yes, but I'd like to tell you...'

'Silence!' said the Inspector. So I gave him what he asked for.

He was still looking at the desk. 'Hello – what's this?' He held up a piece of paper.

At the top was written 6.20.

Plan B

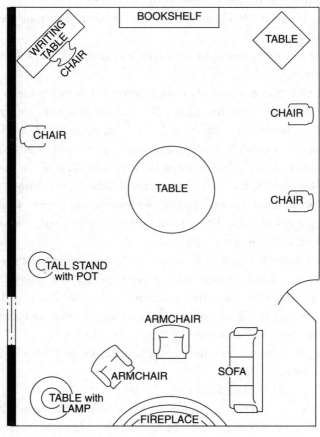

'*Dear Clement*', it began '*Sorry, I cannot wait any longer, but I must...*'

Here the writing ended.

'It's obvious,' said Inspector Slack. 'He sits down to write this, an enemy comes in through the glass door and shoots him.'

'I'd just like to tell...' I began.

'Out of the way, sir. I want to see if there are <u>footprints</u>.' He moved towards the open window.

'I think you ought to know...' I said.

The Inspector turned. 'Now, gentlemen, will you please get out of here.'

We allowed ourselves to be pushed out like children.

'Well,' said Haydock. 'When that bossy little man wants me, you can send him over to the surgery. Goodbye.'

Then Mary came to tell me that Griselda was back, so I went to the sitting room and told her everything. Finally I said, 'The letter is headed 6.20. And the clock fell over and has stopped at 6.22.'

'Yes,' said Griselda. 'But didn't you tell him that the study clock was always kept a quarter of an hour ahead?'

'No,' I said. 'He wouldn't let me.'

'But, Len,' Griselda said, 'that is extraordinary. Because when that clock said twenty past six it was really only five minutes past, and at five minutes past I don't suppose Colonel Protheroe had even arrived at the house.'

CHAPTER 6

We thought that Inspector Slack would come and ask me what it was I had wanted to tell him, so we were surprised when Mary told us that he had gone. Then Griselda said she would go to Old Hall. 'It will be so awful for Anne Protheroe.'

Just after she left, Dennis returned from a tennis party. 'I've always wanted to be right in the middle of a murder,' he said, and went out into the garden to look for footprints. His excitement rather upset me, but death means very little to a boy of sixteen.

An hour later Griselda came back. She had seen Anne Protheroe just after the Inspector had told her the news.

'How did she seem?' I asked.

'She was very quiet...'

'What about Lettice?'

'She was out playing tennis somewhere. But Anne was really very quiet – very strange.'

'The shock?' I suggested.

'I suppose so. And yet, she didn't seem so much shocked as – frightened.'

'Frightened?'

'Yes. I wonder if she knows who killed him. She kept asking if there were any suspects.'

And then Dennis came in full of excitement because of a footprint he had found in one of the flower beds. He was sure that it was very important.

But it was Mary, not Dennis, who brought us the sensational news next morning. We had just sat down to breakfast when she appeared at the door. 'They've arrested Mr Redding!'

'Arrested Lawrence?' cried Griselda. 'It must be some mistake.'

'No mistake,' said Mary. 'Mr Redding went to the police station himself. Last night. He went in, threw down the pistol, and said, "I did it." Just like that.' Satisfied, she left the room.

'It can't be true,' Griselda said. 'What reason could Lawrence have for killing Colonel Protheroe?'

I could have answered that question, but I did not wish to involve Anne Protheroe. 'Remember, I met him just outside the gate. He looked like a mad man. There's the clock, too,' I said. 'Lawrence must have put it back to 6.20 to give himself an <u>alibi</u>. And Inspector Slack believed it.'

'You're wrong. Lawrence knew about that clock being ahead. "Keeping the vicar up to time!" he used to say.'

'He may have forgotten about it.'

'No, if you were committing a murder, you'd be very careful about things like that.'

'You don't know, my dear,' I said. 'You've never done one.'

Before Griselda could reply, a shadow fell across the table, and a very gentle voice said, 'Please forgive me. But after the sad news…' It was Miss Marple. I opened the glass door and she stepped inside and sat down with us. She looked a little pink and a little excited.

'Poor Colonel Protheroe. Not a very pleasant man, but it's still ṣad. And shot in the vicarage study? But you, dear Vicar, were not here at the time?' I explained where I had been.

'Is Dennis not with you this morning?' said Miss Marple.

'Dennis', said Griselda, 'is very excited about a footprint he found, and has gone to tell the police about it.'

'Dear, dear,' said Miss Marple. 'So Dennis thinks he knows who committed the crime. Well, I suppose we all think we know. And I expect everyone thinks it is somebody different. That is why it is so important to have proof. I am sure I know who did it. But I haven't one bit of proof. Inspector Slack said he was coming to see me this morning, but has just phoned to say it won't be necessary.'

'I suppose, that is because of the arrest,' I said.

'The arrest?' Miss Marple leaned forward. 'I didn't know there had been an arrest.'

I said, 'Yes, Lawrence Redding.'

'Lawrence Redding? Now I didn't think...'

'I can't believe it, even now,' Griselda interrupted. 'Even though he has confessed.'

'Confessed?' said Miss Marple. 'Oh, dear! I have been very mistaken...'

'He gave himself up,' said Griselda.

'Oh!' said Miss Marple. 'I am so glad – so very glad.'

'It does show he is truly sorry, I suppose,' I said.

'Sorry?' Miss Marple looked surprised. 'Oh, but Vicar, you don't think that he is guilty?'

'He has confessed...'

'Yes, but that just proves it. I mean that he had nothing to do with it.'

'No,' I said. 'If you have not committed a murder, I cannot see the reason to pretend you have.'

'Oh, of course, there's a reason!' said Miss Marple. 'There's always a reason. And young men are so hot-headed and so quick to believe the worst.'

'If you had seen his face last night...' I began.

'Tell me,' said Miss Marple. I did so. When I had finished she said, 'I know that I am very often rather stupid, but I really do not understand your point. It seems to me that if a young man had decided to take another man's life, he would not appear upset about it afterwards. It is difficult to imagine being in such a position, but I cannot believe I would be upset myself.'

'But if there was an argument,' I argued, 'the shot may have been fired in sudden anger, and Lawrence might have been very upset afterwards about what he had done.'

'But, Mr Clement, it does not seem to me that the facts fit your argument. Your <u>maid</u> said that Mr Redding was only in the house for two minutes. And the Colonel was shot while he was writing a letter. The letter also seems very strange. I mean...' She looked round.

Lettice Protheroe came in through the glass door. 'I hear they've arrested Lawrence.'

'Yes,' said Griselda.

'Have you seen my hat here – a little yellow one?' said Lettice. 'I think I left it in the study.'

'If you did, it's there still,' said Griselda.

'I'll go and see,' said Lettice.

'I'm afraid you can't get it now,' I said. 'Inspector Slack has locked the room.'

'Oh, what a bore!'

'Surely, Lettice, a yellow hat won't be much good to you just now?'

'You mean I should wear black? I won't bother. It's terribly old-fashioned.' A strange smile came to her lips. 'I think I'll go home and tell Anne that Lawrence has been arrested.' She went out of the French window again.

Miss Marple was smiling. 'That child is not half so <u>dreamy</u> as she pretends to be. She's got a very definite idea in her head and she's acting upon it.'

There was a loud knock on the <u>dining room</u> door. 'Colonel Melchett's here,' Mary said. 'He wants to see the master.'

I got up at once.

CHAPTER 7

Colonel Melchett is the <u>Chief Constable</u>[4]. He is small and has red hair. 'Poor old Protheroe,' he said. 'I didn't like him, of course. Nobody did. But I'm shocked at young Redding doing it. And I was surprised when I heard he had confessed.'

'What happened exactly?'

'About ten o'clock last night, Redding comes in, throws down a pistol, and says to the police, "Here I am. I did it." Just like that.'

'Did he describe what happened?' I asked.

'Not much. Said he came here to see you and found Protheroe. They argued and he shot him. Won't say what the argument was about. I've heard gossip[2] – about Redding and the daughter. Was that the trouble?'

'No,' I said. 'It was something very different, but I can't say more just now.'

He nodded. 'Thank you. Well, I've got to see Dr Haydock. He was called out to a patient, but he should be back by now. Like to come along?'

Haydock's house is next door to mine. The doctor had just come in and was eating a plate of eggs and bacon in the dining room. 'Sorry, I had to go out. Babies, not us, decide when they'll arrive. But I've got the bullet for you.' He pushed a little box along the table.

Melchett examined it. 'Point two five?'

Haydock nodded. 'Silly young <u>fellow</u>. Amazing that nobody heard the shot.'

'Yes,' said Melchett.

'The kitchen is on the other side of the house,' I said. 'And the servant was the only person at home.'

'But it's strange,' said Melchett. 'I wonder why Miss Marple didn't hear it. The study window was open.'

'Perhaps she did,' said Haydock.

'No,' I said. 'She didn't say anything about it, and she would have done if she had heard it.'

'What about a <u>silencer</u>? Nobody would hear anything then.'

I noticed that Dr Haydock was looking very cheerful this morning. But he also looked as though he was trying to hide it.

Melchett shook his head. 'Slack didn't find a silencer, and he asked Redding. At first Redding didn't seem to know what he was talking about, and then said he didn't use one. I can't believe he is a murderer.'

'Well, I shall never forget his face when I met him outside my gate, or the way he said, "Oh, you'll see Protheroe all right!" That should have made me suspect what had just happened.'

Haydock stared at me. 'What do you mean – what had just happened? When do you think Redding shot him?'

'A few minutes before I got to the house.'

The doctor shook his head. 'Impossible. He had been dead much longer than that.'

'But, Haydock,' the Colonel said, 'if Redding admits shooting him at a quarter to seven...'

Haydock's face had gone suddenly grey. 'It's impossible. I'm a doctor, and I know. The blood had begun to <u>congeal</u>.'

'But if Redding is lying...' Melchett stopped. 'We'd better go down to the police station and see him.'

CHAPTER 8

Inspector Slack was at the police station and soon we were sitting opposite Lawrence Redding.

'Now,' Melchett said, 'You say you went to the vicarage at about a quarter to seven. You found Protheroe there, argued with him, shot him, and left.'

'Yes. I killed Protheroe.'

'Ah! Well…' Melchett replied. 'How did you manage to have a pistol with you?'

'It was in my pocket.'

'You took it to the vicarage?'

'Yes.'

'Why?'

'I always take it.'

'Why did you change the time of the clock?'

'The clock?' Redding seemed confused.

'Yes, the hands pointed to 6.22.'

'Oh! That – yes. I changed it.'

There was a noise outside. A constable brought in a note. 'For the vicar. It's very urgent.'

I tore it open and read:

Please – please – come to me. I don't know what to do. I want to tell someone. Please come now. And bring anyone you want with you.

Anne Protheroe.

I showed it to Melchett. As we all went out together, I looked over my shoulder and saw Lawrence Redding's face. His eyes were looking at the note in my hand and I have never seen such pain in any human being's face.

As we walked over to Old Hall I told Melchett and Haydock how I had seen Redding and Mrs Protheroe kissing in the studio. When we got there, a man servant opened the door.

'Good morning,' said Melchett. 'Will you tell Mrs Protheroe we are here. Then we would like to ask you a few questions.'

The servant hurried away and returned to say that she would see us soon.

'Now,' said Melchett. 'Was your master here for lunch yesterday?'

'Yes, sir.'

'What happened after lunch?'

'Mrs Protheroe went upstairs for a rest and the Colonel went to his study. Miss Lettice went out to a tennis party. Colonel and Mrs Protheroe had tea at four-thirty. At five-thirty they were driven to the village. Immediately after they had left, Mr Clement rang up and I told him that they had gone out.'

'But Mr Redding did not come to the house yesterday?' said Melchett.

'No, sir.'

'Did anyone else come?'

'Not yesterday.'

'And the day before?'

'Mr Dennis Clement came in the afternoon. And Dr Stone was here. And a lady came in the evening.'

'A lady?' Melchett said. 'Who was she?'

It was a lady the servant had not seen before and she had asked for Colonel Protheroe, not Mrs Protheroe.

'How long did the lady stay?'

Half an hour, he thought. And, yes, he remembered her name now: Mrs Lestrange.

We were very surprised by this. But at that moment a message came that Mrs Protheroe would see us.

Anne was in bed. Her face was pale, but had a strange determined expression.

'Thank you for coming so quickly,' she said. 'Once I had made the decision to tell you, I wanted to do it as soon as possible. So, Colonel Melchett, it was I who killed my husband.'

Colonel Melchett said, 'My dear Mrs Protheroe...'

'It's true! I hated him, and yesterday I shot him.'

'Did you know, Mrs Protheroe, that Lawrence Redding has already confessed to the crime?'

Anne nodded. 'He's in love with me. It was very good of him – but very silly.'

'He knew that it was you who killed your husband?'

'Yes.'

'How did he know?'

She paused, 'I told him... I don't want to talk about it any more.'

'Where did you get the pistol, Mrs Protheroe?'

'The pistol! Oh, it was my husband's. I got it out of the drawer beside his bed.'

'And you took it with you to the vicarage?'

'Yes. I knew he would be there...'

'What time was this?'

'It must have been after six – quarter past – something like that.'

'You took the pistol meaning to shoot your husband?'

'No – meaning to shoot myself. But I went to the study window. I looked in. I saw my husband – and I fired.'

'And then?'

'Then I went away.'

'Did anybody see you entering or leaving the vicarage?'

'Yes. Miss Marple. She was in her garden.' She closed her eyes. 'I've told you everything. Please go now.'

'I'll stay with her,' Dr Haydock whispered to Melchett. 'While you make the necessary arrangements.'

As Melchett and I left the bedroom, I saw a thin man come out of another room along the passage.

'Are you Colonel Protheroe's personal servant?' I asked.

'Yes, sir.'

'Do you know whether he kept a pistol anywhere?'

'I have never seen one.'

'Not in one of the drawers beside his bed?'

The man shook his head. 'He didn't have a pistol. I would have seen it if he had.'

I hurried down the stairs after Melchett. Mrs Protheroe had lied about the pistol.

Why?

CHAPTER 9

After he had left a message at the police station, the Chief Constable said he was going to visit Miss Marple.

'Please can you come with me, Vicar,' he said. 'I don't want to frighten her.'

I smiled. Miss Marple is as strong as any Chief Constable. We rang the bell and were shown by a maid into the sitting room.

When I had introduced Colonel Melchett to Miss Marple, he said, 'I want to talk to you about Colonel Protheroe's death. Your house is next door to the vicarage so perhaps you saw something that would help us.'

'In fact I was in my garden from five o'clock yesterday afternoon and from there, well, I can see everything that is happening next door.'

'I believe that Mrs Protheroe passed by your garden yesterday evening?'

'Yes. At just after a quarter past six. She said she was meeting her husband at the vicarage. She went in by the back gate.'

'And she went inside the vicarage?' Melchett asked.

'Yes. But I suppose Colonel Protheroe wasn't there yet, because she came back almost immediately, and walked down to the studio.'

'I see. And you didn't hear a shot?'

'I didn't hear a shot then,' said Miss Marple.

'But you did hear one?'

'Yes, I think there was a shot somewhere in the woods. Five or ten minutes afterwards. Oh, could it have been…?' She stopped, pale with excitement.

'So, Mrs Protheroe went down to the studio?' said Colonel Melchett.

Plan C

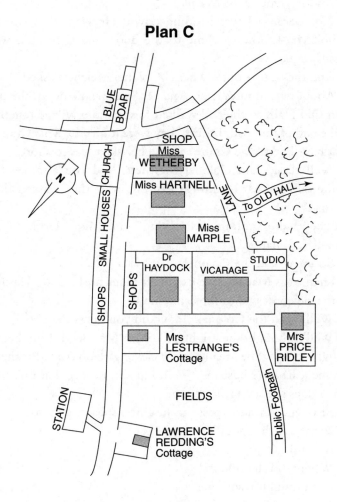

'Yes. Then Mr Redding came to the vicarage gate, looked all round…'

'And saw you, Miss Marple.'

'No. Because I was bending down. He went down to the studio. Mrs Protheroe came to the door, and they both went inside.'

'And they came out – when?' Colonel Melchett asked.

'About ten minutes later. And Dr Stone came down the path from Old Hall, so they all walked towards the village together. At the end of the road, I think they were joined by Miss Cram. It must have been Miss Cram because her skirt was so short.'

'Well then,' said Colonel Melchett, 'did you also see Mrs Protheroe's and Mr Redding's expressions as they walked along the road?'

'They were smiling and talking,' said Miss Marple. 'They seemed very happy.'

'Strange,' said the Colonel.

Then Miss Marple gave us both a shock as she said, 'Has Mrs Protheroe confessed to the crime now?'

'Well!' said the Colonel. 'How did you guess that?'

'Well, I thought she might,' said Miss Marple. 'I think Lettice thought so, too. She's really a very clever girl. So Anne Protheroe says she killed her husband. Well, I'm almost sure that isn't true. When does she say she shot him?'

'At twenty minutes past six. Just after speaking to you.'

'What did she shoot him with?'

'A pistol.'

'Where did she find it?'

'She brought it with her.'

'No,' said Miss Marple. 'She had no gun with her.'

'It might have been in her handbag.'

'She wasn't carrying a handbag.'

'But it all fits together,' Melchett said. 'The time, the overturned clock pointing to 6.22...'

'No,' I interrupted. And I told him about the clock.

Melchett was annoyed. 'Why didn't you tell Slack this last night?'

'Because he wouldn't let me.'

'Nonsense. And if a third person claims to have done this murder, I shall go mad.'

'Colonel Melchett,' Miss Marple said, 'why don't you tell Mr Redding what Mrs Protheroe has done and explain that you don't believe her. And then tell Mrs Protheroe that Mr Redding is innocent – well, then they might both tell you the truth.'

'But they are the only two people who had a reason for killing Protheroe.'

'Oh, do you really think so?'

'Well, can you think of anyone else?'

'Oh, yes!' said Miss Marple. She counted her fingers, 'One, two, three, four, five, six – yes, and a possible seven. I can think of at least seven people who might be very happy to have Colonel Protheroe dead.'

'Seven people? In St Mary Mead?' Melchett said.

Miss Marple nodded brightly. 'There is a lot of wickedness in the world. A good soldier like you doesn't know about these things.'

I thought the Chief Constable was going to explode with anger.

CHAPTER 10

As I entered the vicarage, I could hear voices. I opened the sitting room door and on the sofa beside Griselda, sat Gladys Cram, Dr Stone's secretary.

'Good morning, Mr Clement,' she said. 'Isn't the news awful? A murder! In this quiet village.'

'So Gladys came round to find out all about it,' Griselda said.

Miss Cram laughed loudly. 'A girl also wants a bit of excitement. And, Mrs Clement, you are the only person in the village I can talk to, except a lot of old women.'

'There's Lettice Protheroe,' I said.

She shook her head. 'She's too grand to talk to a girl who has to work to earn money. Although I did hear her saying she wanted to work herself. She's not very happy at home. Well, who would be happy with a stepmother? I wouldn't put up with it.'

'Ah! but you're strong,' said Griselda.

Miss Cram was obviously pleased. 'That's me. And I've told Dr Stone that I must have regular times off. These scientists, they think a girl's a kind of machine. Dr Stone thinks only about archaeology.'

'Is he at the barrow now?' asked Griselda.

Miss Cram shook her head. 'He's not very well this morning. But do tell me, Mr Clement, what do the police think about the murder?'

'Well,' I said, 'things are a little uncertain.'

'Ah! Then they don't think Lawrence Redding did it. So good-looking, isn't he? Like a film star. I couldn't believe it when I heard the police had arrested him. They're very stupid, aren't they?'

'Mr Redding came in and confessed,' I said.

'Why? What did he kill Protheroe for?'

'It's not certain that he did kill him.'

'But why would he say he had done it if he hadn't?'

I could think of no answer to this.

'Well,' she got up, 'I suppose I must go.' And with many thanks and goodbyes, she left.

So I told Griselda everything that had happened that morning, then rang the bell for Mary. When she came in I asked her, 'Mary, are you sure you didn't hear the shot yesterday evening?'

'The shot that killed old Protheroe? No, of course I didn't. If I had, I would have gone in to see what had happened.'

'Yes, but did you hear any other shot – one down in the woods, perhaps?'

'Oh! That.' Mary paused. 'Just one. Strange sort of noise it was.'

'What time did you hear it?'

'I don't know.'

'Was it long before Mr Redding came?'

'No. Ten minutes – a quarter of an hour – not longer than that.'

I nodded.

'Is that all?' said Mary. 'Because the potatoes are probably burning.'

'Yes, you can go.' She left the room, and I turned to Griselda. 'Don't you think it would be a good idea if Mary was taught how to cook?'

'No. If she learned to cook, she would leave to get more money. So while Mary can't cook we're safe, because nobody else would want her. Also,' continued Griselda, 'you must forgive her for not caring about Colonel Protheroe's death. Because he sent her boyfriend to prison.'

'What for?'

'For <u>poaching</u>. You know, that man, Archer. Mary has been with him for two years.'

'I didn't know that.'

'Darling Len, you never know anything.'

'It's strange,' I said, 'that everyone says the shot came from the woods.'

'It's not strange at all,' said Griselda. 'One often hears shots in the woods. So when you hear a shot, you naturally think it comes from there.'

The door opened again. 'Colonel Melchett's back,' said Mary. 'And that police inspector. They're in the study.'

As soon as I went in, Melchett said, 'Inspector Slack does not believe that Redding is innocent.'

'If he didn't do it, why did he say that he did?' said Slack.

'But Mrs Protheroe did exactly the same.'

'That's different. She's a woman, and women act in that silly way. She heard he had confessed, so made up a story. But Redding's a man. And if he says he did it, well, then he did.'

'Miss Marple saw him and Mrs Protheroe leave the studio just after six-thirty. Dr Stone met them and they walked together to the village. Mrs Protheroe then went into Miss Hartnell's house to borrow a gardening magazine. Miss Hartnell says she stayed there until seven o'clock, and Redding went with Stone to the Blue Boar for a drink. Then he went back to the vicarage and asked for the vicar at the front door. Mary told him that Colonel Protheroe was there, so he went in – and shot him – just as he said he did!'

Melchett shook his head. 'But the doctor says that Protheroe was shot before six-thirty.'

'Oh, doctors, what do they know!' Slack replied.

'But I touched the body and it was cold,' I said.

'And why should I believe you?' said Slack. 'When you did not tell me the truth about your clock.'

'I tried to tell you several times,' I said. 'And you refused to listen.'

'Nonsense. And anyway, why do you keep your clock a quarter of an hour ahead?'

'It is supposed,' I said, 'to help me to be on time.'

'Inspector,' said Colonel Melchett. 'What we want is the true story from both Mrs Protheroe and Mr Redding. I have asked

Dr Haydock to bring Mrs Protheroe over here. But I think we should see Redding first.'

'I'll call the station,' said Slack, 'and then we'll get to work on this room.'

I decided to leave them and found my wife and Miss Marple in the sitting room.

'I wish you could solve the crime, Miss Marple,' Griselda said. 'Like you did when Miss Wetherby's bag of onions disappeared. And all because it reminded you of something very different, something about a bag of wood for the fire.'

'You are laughing at me,' said Miss Marple, 'but that is a very good way of finding the truth. It's what people call intuition. Intuition is like reading a word without having to spell it out. You know the word because you've seen it so often before. Do you understand, Vicar?'

'Yes,' I said. 'If a thing reminds you of something else – well, it's probably the same type of thing.'

'Exactly.'

'And what does the murder of Colonel Protheroe remind you of?'

Miss Marple sighed. 'So many things. For example, there was Major Hargreaves, a respected churchwarden. And all the time he was keeping a second family – a former servant, and five children! What a terrible shock to his wife and daughter.'

'I wish you would tell me', I said, 'who your seven suspects are.'

'Oh, but I mustn't mention names. You can think of them yourself, I am sure.'

'I can't. There is Lettice Protheroe, I suppose, because she probably gets money after her father's death. But I can't think of anyone else.'

'I don't believe that it was Lawrence or Anne, or Lettice,' Griselda said. 'There must be some clue that would help us.'

'There is the note, of course,' said Miss Marple.

'It seems to fix the time of his death exactly,' I said. 'And yet, is that possible? Mrs Protheroe would only have just left the study. She would not have had time to reach the studio.'

'What do you think, Miss Marple?' asked Griselda.

'I wasn't thinking about the time on the letter. What I find strange, is what it said.'

'I don't understand,' I said. 'Colonel Protheroe just wrote that he couldn't wait any longer...'

'At twenty minutes past six?' said Miss Marple. 'Mary had told him that you wouldn't be in till half past six, and he was willing to wait until then. And yet at twenty past six he sits down and says he "can't wait any longer".'

I looked at the old lady, feeling increased respect for her intelligence.

'Imagine,' I said, 'that at about 6.30 Colonel Protheroe sat down to write that he couldn't wait any longer. And as he was writing, someone came in through the garden doors, came up behind the Colonel and shot him. Then he saw the note and the clock and he wrote 6.20 at the top of the letter and altered the clock to 6.22. He thought that it gave him a perfect alibi.'

'Then there was that shot I heard,' said Miss Marple. 'Yes, the sound was different from the usual sort of shot.'

'Louder?' I suggested.

No, Miss Marple didn't think it had been louder, just different. Then she got up and said she really must get home.

CHAPTER 12

When Lawrence Redding arrived I was called to the study.

'We want to ask you a few questions, here where it happened,' Colonel Melchett said. 'Did you know that someone else has also confessed to the murder which you say you committed?' The effect of these words on Lawrence was immediate. 'Someone else? Who – who?'

'Mrs Protheroe,' said Colonel Melchett.

'Nonsense. It's impossible.'

'Well, we do not believe her story either,' said Melchett. 'And Dr Haydock is certain that the murder could not have been committed at the time you say you did it. So, why don't you tell us the truth?'

'I've been a fool,' Lawrence said. 'How could I have thought for one minute that Anne did it? I met her in the studio that afternoon...' He paused.

'We know all about that,' said Melchett.

'Right. Well, after the vicar saw us there, I promised him that I would leave the village. So I met Mrs Protheroe that evening at a quarter past six and told her my decision. Then we left the studio, and met Dr Stone, and I went off with him to the Blue Boar for a drink. I was upset and afterwards I suddenly decided to go and see the vicar.

'At the front door, I was told that he was out, but that Colonel Protheroe was in the study waiting for him. So I said I'd wait, too.' He stopped.

'Well?' said Colonel Melchett.

'Protheroe was sitting at the desk. He was dead. Then I saw the pistol lying on the floor beside him. I picked it up – and recognized it as my pistol! And I just thought Anne must have taken it, meaning to shoot herself because she was so unhappy. I thought that after we said goodbye in the village, she must have come back here and – so I put the pistol in my pocket and left. Just outside the gate, I met the vicar. He said something nice and normal about seeing Protheroe – and I just started shouting. Then I walked and walked. And I thought that if Anne had done this awful thing, I was responsible, so I went and confessed.'

The Colonel said, 'Did you touch the body?'

'No. I could see he was dead without touching him.'

'Did you see a note on the desk?'

'No.'

'Did you touch the clock?'

'No. I remember a clock lying there, but I did not touch it.'

'When did you last see your pistol?'

Lawrence Redding thought. 'I'm not sure.'

'Where do you keep it?'

'On a shelf in my cottage.'

'Who has been to your cottage lately?'

'Oh! Crowds of people. I had a tea party the day before yesterday. Lettice Protheroe, Dennis, and all their friends. And then some of the old ladies often come in.'

'Do you lock the cottage up when you go out?'

'No. No one locks their house up round here.'

'Who cleans your cottage?'

'Old Mrs Archer comes in every morning.'

'Would she remember when she last saw the pistol?'

'I don't know.'

'So, almost anyone might have taken it.'

The door opened and Dr Haydock came in with Anne Protheroe.

'Forgive me, Anne,' Lawrence said. 'It was awful of me to think you could have killed...'

She turned to Colonel Melchett. 'Is it true, what Dr Haydock told me?'

'That Mr Redding is not a suspect any more? Yes. So what about your story, Mrs Protheroe?'

'I suppose you think I was foolish?'

'Well, let us forget about that. What I want now is the truth.'

She nodded. 'I had arranged to meet Lawrence that evening at the studio. At a quarter past six. My husband and I drove into the village together. He said that he was going to see the vicar. I was rather worried about meeting Lawrence in the garden while my husband was inside the vicarage.

'But I thought that perhaps my husband wouldn't stay very long. To find this out, I came along the back road to the study. I hoped no one would see me, but of course Miss Marple was in her garden! She stopped me and I explained I was going to meet my husband. Then I went straight across to the study and looked through the window. The room was empty. So I hurried down to the studio where Lawrence joined me.'

'You say the room was empty, Mrs Protheroe?'

'Yes.'

'Very strange.'

Inspector Slack whispered to the Chief Constable, who nodded.

'Do you mind, Mrs Protheroe, just showing us exactly what you did?' Inspector Slack pushed open the glass doors, and she stepped outside and walked round the house to the left. Then he told me to go and sit at the desk. As I sat there, I heard someone outside. They paused there for a minute, then went away. Inspector Slack told me to return to the other side of the room. Mrs Protheroe came back through the glass door.

'Is that exactly what you did?' Colonel Melchett asked her.

'Yes.'

'Then can you tell us where the vicar was in the room?' asked Inspector Slack.

'But I didn't see him.'

Inspector Slack nodded. 'He was round the corner at the desk. And that's why you didn't see your husband.'

'Oh! Was he sitting there when he was killed?'

'Yes, Mrs Protheroe. He was. Did you know that Mr Redding had a pistol?'

'Yes.'

'Did you know where he kept it?'

'I think I saw it on a shelf in his cottage.'

'When was the last time you were at the cottage, Mrs Protheroe?'

'About three weeks ago. Mr Redding usually came up to the Hall. He was painting a picture of Lettice. We – we often met in the woods afterwards.'

Colonel Melchett nodded.

'It's so awful – having to tell you these things,' she cried. 'And we did nothing wrong. We were just friends. That was all.'

'Thank you, Mrs Protheroe, for answering my questions,' he said.

'Then – can I go?'

'Yes.'

So she and Haydock and Lawrence Redding left. Colonel Melchett remained, and Slack who was looking at the note. It was then that I told him Miss Marple's theory.

'Oh,' Slack said, 'I believe the old lady's right. Look, the time is written in blue ink!'

We were all rather excited.

'You've examined the note for <u>fingerprints</u>, of course,' said Melchett.

'Of course. No fingerprints on the note at all. Fingerprints on the pistol are Lawrence Redding's.'

'Who lives in the other house next door?' the Colonel suddenly asked.

'Mrs Price Ridley.'

'We'll go and see her. She might know something.'

As we left the vicarage, Dennis came running towards us. 'What about that footprint I found?' he said to the Inspector.

'It was the gardener's,' said Inspector Slack.

'You don't think it might be someone else wearing the gardener's boots?'

'No, I don't!'

'You're not arresting Uncle Len, are you?' asked Dennis.

'Why should I?' asked Slack.

'Because only the day before the crime he said that any one who murdered Colonel Protheroe would be doing the world a favour.'

'Ah!' said Inspector Slack, 'that explains something Mary said when I spoke to her. Come on, Clement.'

'Where are you going? Can I come, too?' asked Dennis.

'No, you can't,' I said. We left him looking after us with a hurt expression.

We went up to the neat front door of Mrs Price Ridley's house and the inspector rang the bell. A pretty servant answered the door.

'Is Mrs Price Ridley in?' asked Melchett.

'No, sir. She's gone down to the police station.'

As we left, Melchett said, 'If she's gone to confess to the murder, too, I really shall go mad.'

CHAPTER 13

We discovered Mrs Price Ridley talking very fast to a patient policeman.

She stopped when she saw us. 'Ah! I am glad you are taking action after what happened. Shocking, it was!'

'Well, have you anything you can tell us about it?' Melchett asked.

'It's your job to tell me.'

'We're doing our best, Mrs Price Ridley,' said the Chief Constable.

'But this man hadn't even heard of it till I told him!' she cried.

We all looked at the policeman. 'The lady was called on the telephone,' he said. 'Bad language was used.'

'Oh! I see,' Colonel Melchett said. 'You came down here to make a complaint.'

Mrs Price Ridley began talking again. 'I was telephoned in my own house and insulted!'

'When?'

'Yesterday evening. About half past six. And I was threatened...'

'What did they threaten you with?'

'I can't remember.'

'Was it a man's voice or a woman's?'

'It was an unpleasant voice,' said Mrs Price Ridley. 'Now deep, now high. A very strange voice.'

'Probably a joke,' said the Colonel. 'But can you tell me exactly what was said?'

Mrs Price Ridley thought about it. 'You promise to tell no one outside this room?'

'Of course.'

'Well, this person began by saying, "You are a very unpleasant old woman who tells lies!" Me, Colonel Melchett! "And now the police are after you."'

'Of course, you were upset,' said Melchett, trying not to smile.

'"Unless you keep quiet, it will be very bad for you." I replied, "Who are you?" and the voice answered, "The <u>Avenger</u>". I gave a little cry. And the person laughed! Then they put down the telephone. I thought I was going to faint. So when I heard a shot in the woods, I…'

'A shot in the woods?' asked Inspector Slack.

'Yes. Like a very big gun. I had to lie down on the sofa.'

'Shocking,' said Melchett. 'And the shot was loud? As though it was close by?'

'Perhaps because I was upset.'

'What time was this?'

'About half past six.'

'Well,' said Melchett. 'We'll see what we can find out for you.'

'Just think of the call as a joke, and don't worry, Mrs Price Ridley,' I said.

She looked at me coldly. Obviously she was still cross about the missing pound note. And, shaking her head, she left.

'So, that is three people who heard the shot,' said Inspector Slack. 'We've now got to find out who fired it. But first I'm going to investigate that telephone call.'[5]

'Mrs Price Ridley's?'

The Inspector smiled. 'No. I meant the call that got you out of the vicarage. And the next thing is to find out what everyone was doing that evening between six and seven. We'll begin with you, Mr Clement.'

'Oh. Well, the telephone call was at about half past five.'

'A man's voice, or a woman's?'

'A woman's, I think. But I thought it was Mrs Abbott speaking.'

'And you left immediately? How long did it take you?'

'It's nearly two miles. So…'

'And where was Mrs Clement?'

'She was in London. She arrived back by the 6.50 train.'

'Right. That finishes with the vicarage. I'll be off to Old Hall next. And then I want to talk to Mrs Lestrange. Why did she go to see Protheroe the night before he was killed?'

CHAPTER 14

On my way home, Dr Haydock stopped his car beside me just outside his house. 'I've taken Mrs Protheroe home,' he called. 'Come in a minute.'

So I did. As we sat down I told him that we now knew the time of the shot.

'That clears Anne Protheroe,' he said. 'Well, I'm glad it's neither of those two. I like them both.'

I believed him, and yet I wondered why he now looked so unhappy. This morning he had looked like a man free from worry. Suddenly he said, 'I meant to tell you about your curate, Hawes. All this trouble made me forget.'

'Is he ill?'

'Not exactly. You know, of course, that he has had sleeping sickness?'

'No,' I said. 'I didn't. When did he have it?'

'About a year ago. He got better. But it's a strange illness – the whole character may change after it.'

'Haydock,' I said, 'if you knew that someone was a murderer, would you tell the police, or would you stay silent?'

He turned on me angrily. 'Why do you ask me that?'

'Well, as a doctor, if you somehow discovered the truth – I wondered what you would do, that's all.'

His anger disappeared. 'I hope I would do my duty, Clement.'

'But which of those choices do you think would be your duty?'

He looked at me. 'Every man has to decide for himself.'

'Well, I must be going,' I said. 'I'm already late for lunch.'

My family demanded a full account of the morning's activities, when I arrived. But then Mary came in: 'Mr Hawes wants to see you. I've put him in the sitting room.' Then she handed me a note. I tore it open and read:

Dear Mr Clement,

I would be very grateful if you could come and see me this afternoon. I am in great trouble and would like your advice.

Sincerely yours,
Estelle Lestrange.

CHAPTER 15

Hawes was shaking all over. I told him he should be in bed but he said that he was perfectly well. 'I called to tell you how sorry I was that such a death has happened in the vicarage. But they haven't arrested Mr Redding?'

'No,' I said. 'That was all a mistake.'

'Why? Do the police suspect someone else? Colonel Protheroe was not a popular man. But murder! For murder – one would need a very strong reason.'

'I suppose so.'

'Have you told the police about that man Archer threatening Protheroe?'

'No,' I said. 'I have not.'

'I <u>overheard</u> Protheroe telling you yesterday. So I hope you will.'

I was silent. Archer is a poacher, but friendly and cheerful. He was probably very angry about being sent to prison but would feel differently when he came out.

'If he shot Colonel Protheroe...'

'If! There is no evidence of any kind that he did.'

'I don't understand you, sir.'

'Don't you,' I said. 'But you're young. When you get to my age, you will find that you like to think the best of people.'

'I just wondered... if Colonel Protheroe had told you something...'

'Nothing that you didn't hear.'

Hawes was nervous and his behaviour strange. I remembered what Dr Haydock had said about his illness and supposed that explained it. He left unwillingly, as though he had more to say but didn't know how to say it. And then I also left to go and see Mrs Lestrange.

In the sitting room Mrs Lestrange rose to meet me. There was something dead about her face. Only the eyes were alive. There was a <u>watchful</u> look in them. We sat down.

'It was very good of you to come, Mr Clement. I wanted to talk to you the other day. Then I decided not to. I was wrong. I am in a very strange position, Mr Clement, and I want to ask your advice about what I should do next. What is past is past and cannot be undone. You understand?'

Before I could reply, the maid came in. 'There is a police inspector here, and he says he must see you.' Mrs Lestrange said calmly, 'Show him in, Hilda.'

Slack strode in. 'Good afternoon, madam.' Then he saw me and <u>frowned</u>. Mrs Lestrange took no notice. 'What can I do for you, Inspector?'

'Murder of Colonel Protheroe. I'm asking everyone where they were yesterday evening between the hours of six and seven p.m.'

'I was here. In this house.'

'Oh! And your maid was here too?'

'No, it was Hilda's afternoon out. So, you will have to trust me,' said Mrs Lestrange, smiling.

'You were at home all afternoon?'

'You said between six and seven, Inspector. I went out for a walk earlier. I returned some time before five o'clock.'

'Then if a lady – Miss Hartnell perhaps – said that she came here about six o'clock, rang the bell, but got no answer – you would say she was mistaken?'

'Oh, no. If your maid is in, she can say you are not at home. If you are alone and do not want to see people – well, the only thing to do is to let them ring.'

Inspector Slack looked confused.

'Miss Hartnell is very boring,' said Mrs Lestrange. 'She rang at least six times before she went away.'

'So if anyone said that they'd seen you out and about then…'

'Oh! But they didn't, did they? Because I was in, you see.'

'Exactly, madam.' The Inspector moved his chair a little nearer. 'I understand that you visited Colonel Protheroe the night before his death.'

'Yes.'

'Can you tell me what you talked about?'

'It was private.'

'I'm afraid I must ask you to tell me about it, private or not.'

'But I shall not tell you. I will only say that nothing which was discussed had anything to do with the crime.'

'I don't think you are the best judge of that.'

'Then again, you will have to trust me, Inspector.'

Inspector Slack's face was suddenly very red. 'This is a serious matter, Mrs Lestrange. I want the truth!' He banged his hand on a table.

Mrs Lestrange said nothing.

'Did you know Colonel Protheroe well?'

There was a pause before she said, 'I had not seen him for several years.'

'It was an unusual time to call on him.'

'No, it wasn't. I wanted to see him alone.'

'Why didn't you want to see Mrs or Miss Protheroe?'

'That, Inspector, is my business.'

Inspector Slack got up. 'Good afternoon, madam. But remember we are going to find out the truth.'

When he had gone Mrs Lestrange also got up and held out her hand to me. 'I am going to send you away. It is too late for advice now.' Then she turned away. 'I know what I must do.'

Chapter 16

I had arranged to visit Mrs Protheroe to discuss the funeral arrangements, so I walked to Old Hall.

When we had finished, I said goodbye and took the private path towards the vicarage. I had a plan. When I found a place where the plants beside the path looked as though someone had walked on them, I left the path and forced my way through. But suddenly I heard someone else moving very close to me. As I paused, Lawrence Redding appeared, carrying a large stone.

I must have looked shocked, for he started to laugh. 'No,' he said, 'it's not a clue, it's a gift.'

'What?'

'I wanted an excuse to call on Miss Marple. And I heard that she loves old stones for her Japanese garden.'

'True,' I said. 'But why do you want to see her?'

'Well, if there was anything to be seen yesterday evening, Miss Marple saw it. Clement, I'm going to solve this crime. For Anne's sake.' He paused, then said, 'What are you doing in the woods, Vicar?' I didn't know what to say.

'We've got the same idea, haven't we?' he smiled. 'How did the murderer come to the study? First way, along the road and through the gate. Second way, by the front door. Third way – is there a third way? My idea was to see if any of the bushes were broken near the vicarage garden wall.'

'That was just my idea,' I admitted.

'But I suddenly thought that I'd like to see Miss Marple first.'

So we walked together to her house. She was working in the garden, and was very pleased with the stone. 'It's so kind of you, Mr Redding.'

Then Lawrence asked his most important question. But Miss Marple was sure she had seen nobody in the road when he and Anne were in the studio.

'Did you see anyone go by the path into the woods that afternoon?' I asked. 'Or come from there?'

'Oh, yes. Dr Stone and Miss Cram – it's the quickest way to the barrow. That was just after two o'clock. And Dr Stone returned that way – as you know, Mr Redding, because he joined you and Mrs Protheroe.'

'And that shot,' I said. 'The one you heard, Miss Marple. Mr Redding and Mrs Protheroe must have heard it, too.'

'Yes,' Lawrence said. 'I believe I did hear some shots.'

'I only heard one,' said Miss Marple.

'I can't remember it very well,' said Lawrence. 'All I could think about was Anne –'

Miss Marple changed the subject. 'Inspector Slack asked me whether I heard the shot after Mr Redding and Mrs Protheroe had left the studio or before. I believe that it was after.'

'Then it couldn't have been Dr Stone,' said Lawrence. 'Although nobody has ever thought that he did shoot Protheroe.'

'Ah!' said Miss Marple. 'But I always think it wise to suspect everybody just a little.'

'Well then,' said Lawrence. 'Can you think why Mrs Lestrange visited Protheroe after dinner on Wednesday night?'

'No, but I expect someone heard something. Perhaps, Mr Redding, you can find out. Women servants hate talking to the police. But a nice-looking young man, I'm sure they would tell him at once.'

'I'll go and try this evening,' said Lawrence. 'But first, the vicar and I have a little job to do.' So we said goodbye to Miss Marple and walked back to the woods.

We went up the path until we came to a new place where it looked as though someone had left the path on the right-hand side. We turned and walked this way, but after a short distance there were no more broken bushes. So we went back to the path and walked a little farther along it. Again we came to a place where the bushes looked broken. This time we went towards the vicarage and finally to where the bushes grew against the wall.

Then suddenly there was the sound of breaking wood. I pushed forward – and came face to face with Inspector Slack.

'So it's you,' he said. 'What are you both doing here?' A little ashamed, we explained.

'Exactly,' said the Inspector. 'I had the same idea. Would you like to know something?'

'Yes,' I said.

'Whoever murdered Colonel Protheroe did not come this way! There's no sign that anyone climbed over this wall. Whoever shot the Colonel came through the front door. There's no other way he could have come.'

'Impossible,' I cried.

'Why impossible?' he said. 'Your door is open. Anyone can walk in. They know you are out. They know Mrs Clement is in London. They know Dennis is at a tennis party. And they don't need to come through the village. Just opposite the vicarage gate is a public footpath. Yes, that's the way the person came.'

And it really seemed that he must be right.

CHAPTER 17

Inspector Slack came round to see me the next morning. 'Well, sir,' he said. 'I've found out about that telephone call that you received.'[5]

'And?'

'It's rather strange. It was put through from the North <u>Lodge</u> of Old Hall. The place is empty but a window was open. There were no fingerprints on the telephone because it had been cleaned. That tells us something.'

'What?'

'It shows that call was made deliberately to get you out of the house. So the murder was planned. If the call had just been a joke, the fingerprints would not have been wiped off so carefully.'

'I understand.'

'And I've found out something else. You remember Mrs Price Ridley's complaint about that call to her house?'

'Yes?'

'Well, we tracked it – and do you know where it came from? Mr Lawrence Redding's cottage!'

'What?' I said.

'But it wasn't Mr Redding who made the call. At that time, 6.30, he was on his way to the Blue Boar with Dr Stone. So, someone walked into the empty cottage and used the telephone. That's two strange telephone calls in one day, and I bet they were made by the same person.'

'Why?'

'Well, first Mr Redding's pistol. Then his telephone. Someone's trying to make him look guilty.'

'So why was the first call not made from his cottage?' I asked.

'Ah, what did Mr Redding do most afternoons? He went up to Old Hall and painted Miss Protheroe's picture. And from his cottage he would go through the North Gate. Now you see why the call was made from there.'

I thought for a moment. 'Were there any fingerprints on Mr Redding's phone?'

'There were not,' said the Inspector crossly. 'That old woman who cleans for him wiped them off yesterday morning. But if only that shot hadn't come just at the end of the call – well, I'd know where to look.'

'Where?'

'Well, what about the lady who called on Colonel Protheroe the night before the murder?'

'Mrs Lestrange!' I cried.

'Yes,' the Inspector said. 'Suppose Mrs Lestrange had successfully <u>blackmailed</u> Protheroe in the past. Then, years later, she hears that he is living in this village, so comes down here and tries it again. But perhaps this time he says he will go to the police. So she kills him.'

I said, 'Inspector, Mrs Lestrange is not the kind of person to blackmail someone. She's – well, she's a lady.'

'Well, sir, you are a vicar,' he said. 'So you don't know much about the world. Lady indeed! That woman could push a knife into you without feeling anything.'

Strangely, I could imagine Mrs Lestrange doing that, but not blackmail.

'But, of course, she can't have telephoned Mrs Price Ridley and shot Colonel Protheroe at exactly the same time,' he continued. Then suddenly he shouted, 'Got it! That telephone call was an alibi. She knew we'd connect it with the first one, so she paid some village boy to make the call for her. And I'm going to find out who.'

The Inspector hurried off.

'Miss Marple wants to see you,' said Griselda, appearing at the door. 'She sent over a very strange note. For some reason she can't leave her house. Do go and find out why.'

I found Miss Marple in a very excited state. 'My nephew, Raymond West, is coming here today,' she explained. 'He writes very clever books, though in real life people are not nearly so unpleasant as he makes his characters. Clever young men know so little about life.'

'Was there was something you wanted to see me about?' I asked.

'Oh! Of course. I had forgotten. Yes. It was about a strange thing that happened last night. I couldn't sleep because I kept thinking about Colonel Protheroe, so I got up and looked out of my window. And what do you think I saw?'

'I don't know.'

'Gladys Cram,' said Miss Marple. 'Going into the woods with a suitcase.'

'A suitcase?'

'Yes. Why would she take a suitcase into the woods at twelve o'clock at night? I don't expect it has anything to do with the murder. But it is a Strange Thing. And just now we must all take notice of Strange Things.'

'Perhaps she was going to sleep in the barrow?' I suggested.

'She didn't,' said Miss Marple. 'Because a short time afterwards she came back, and she didn't have the suitcase with her.'

CHAPTER 18

The <u>inquest</u>[6] into Colonel Protheroe's death was held that same Saturday afternoon at the Blue Boar.

Lawrence Redding told how he had found the body, and admitted that the pistol belonged to him.

Mrs Protheroe said that she had last seen her husband at about a quarter to six when they left each other in the village street. She had gone to the vicarage at about a quarter past six and thought that the study was empty. But later she had realized that if her husband had been sitting at the desk, she would not have seen him.

I gave evidence next. I told of my appointment with Protheroe and the phone call asking me to go to the Abbotts' house. I described how I had found the body.

'How many people, Mr Clement, knew that Colonel Protheroe was coming to see you that evening?' the <u>coroner</u>[6] asked.

'My wife knew, and my nephew Dennis, and Colonel Protheroe himself mentioned it that morning in the village. Several people must have heard, as he spoke very loudly.'

Dr Haydock then described the appearance of the body and the exact injuries. It was his opinion that the Colonel had been shot at approximately 6.20 to 6.30 – certainly not later than 6.35.

Inspector Slack's evidence was careful and short. The unfinished letter was produced and the time on it – 6.20 – noted. And because of the clock, it was thought that the time of death was 6.22.

Our servant, Mary, was next. She said she hadn't heard anything. Colonel Protheroe had arrived at a quarter past six exactly. She heard the church clock just after she had shown him into the study. She didn't hear any shot. Well, of course, there must have been a shot, because the gentleman was found shot – but she had not heard it.

Mrs Lestrange had been asked to give evidence, but a medical certificate, signed by Dr Haydock, said that she was too ill to attend.

The last person to give evidence was Mrs Archer, who cleaned Lawrence Redding's cottage. She recognized the pistol. She had seen it in Mr Redding's sitting room. The last time she had seen it was on the day of the murder at lunchtime when she left.

I was surprised. The inspector had told me she wasn't sure of the time when he questioned her, but she was sure now.

The verdict was given almost immediately: Murder by Person or Persons Unknown.

As I left, I saw a group of young men with bright, interested faces waiting outside. So I went straight back into the Blue Boar and was lucky enough to see Dr Stone.

'Newspaper reporters,' I said. 'Could I wait here with you for a while?'

'Of course, Mr Clement.'

He led the way upstairs and into his sitting room, where Miss Cram was working. She gave me a wide smile. 'Awful, isn't it? Not knowing who did it.'

'Were you there?' I asked Dr Stone.

'No, I have no interest in such things. I only think about archaeology.'

'It must be very interesting,' I said.

This was just what he wanted to hear. Immediately he began to explain why it was so interesting.

Dr Stone was a little man. His head was round and bald, and he wore thick glasses. He soon began to explain his disagreement with Colonel Protheroe.

'A very stupid man. Because he had read a few books, he thought he knew more than a man who has studied the subject all his life and...'

'You'll miss your train if you are not careful,' interrupted Gladys.

'Oh!' He looked at his watch. 'This is a wonderful girl, Mr Clement. She never forgets anything.' He went into the next room and returned with a suitcase.

'I'm going up to London for two days, to see my mother, and my lawyers. On Tuesday I shall return.' Dr Stone attempted to leave, carrying the suitcase, as well as a large coat and a bag of books. I rushed to help him. And so we walked together to the station, Dr Stone with the suitcase, and I with the coat and books.

'Goodness,' Dr Stone suddenly cried. 'The train!'

A train from London was standing in the station and the train for London was just coming in. We began to run, and inside we <u>bumped into</u> a very good-looking young man. I recognized him immediately as Miss Marple's nephew and I apologized. But he was not pleased. Dr Stone climbed on the train just before it started.

I began to walk back to the village and our local chemist, Mr Cherabim, joined me. 'He was lucky not to miss his train,' he said. 'But you can never be sure they will be on time. Do you know last Thursday — the day of the murder — I had been to a meeting in London. And the 6.50 train was half an hour late! I didn't get home until half past seven.'

'Annoying,' I said. Then I saw Lawrence Redding on the other side of the road, and told Mr Cherabim that I had to speak to him.

CHAPTER 19

'I am very glad to see you,' said Lawrence. 'Would you like to come to my cottage?'

We went up the path, and he took a key from his pocket.

'You keep the door locked now,' I said.

'Yes. Someone knew about that pistol of mine.' He opened the door and I went inside. 'That means that the murderer must have been inside this house – perhaps even had a drink with me.'

'Not necessarily,' I replied. 'The whole village probably knows where you keep your socks.' Then suddenly I asked, 'Was the pistol <u>loaded</u>?'

Lawrence shook his head. 'But there was a box of bullets beside it. Unless the real murderer is found I shall be the suspect until I die. But let me tell you about last night.'

He had, following Miss Marple's advice, gone up to Old Hall and talked to the servant, Rose.

'It's about Colonel Protheroe's death,' he had said to her. 'I feel that someone might have seen or heard something, and I wondered if you could help me?'

'Yes, sir?'

I can imagine that Lawrence must have looked very attractive, with his blue eyes shining.

'So can you tell me anything about the lady who called to see Colonel Protheroe the night before he died.'

'Mrs Lestrange?'

'Yes.'

'Well, Gladdie said—'

'Gladdie?'

'Gladdie's a kitchen servant.'

'So what did she say?'

'Oh, nothing! We were just talking.'

Lawrence looked at her. 'I wonder what Mrs Lestrange wanted to see Colonel Protheroe about. Rose, if Gladdie overheard something – it might not seem important – I'd be so grateful to you.'

'Well, she was walking past the study window, and the master was there with the lady. And of course he did talk very loud.'

'Of course,' said Lawrence, 'She couldn't avoid overhearing. Can I go into the kitchen and speak to her?'

'Oh, no, sir!' Rose cried. 'She doesn't want anyone else to know.'

At last a meeting was arranged in the garden, and here Lawrence spoke to a very nervous Gladdie. 'I didn't hear much,' she told him.

'I understand.'

'Well, the master was very angry. "After all these years" – that's what he said – "you dare to come here." Then he said, "I refuse. You will not see her. I will not allow it." It sounded as though the lady wanted to tell Mrs Protheroe something, and he didn't want her to. And I thought, "Men are all alike. Even Colonel Protheroe, a churchwarden and…"'

'Did you hear anything else?'

'He said, "I don't believe it. Whatever Dr Haydock says, I don't believe it."'

'Did you hear the lady speak at all?'

'Only at the end. She said, "By this time tomorrow night, you may be dead." So when I heard about the murder, I said to Rose, "It's her who did it!"'

I thought of Miss Marple's churchwarden with his second secret family. Was this the same situation? I also wondered about

Haydock. He had saved Mrs Lestrange from giving evidence at the inquest. Perhaps he suspected her of the crime and was trying to protect her. But something in me said, 'It can't be her!' Why? And then something else replied, 'Because she's a very attractive woman. That's why.'

CHAPTER 20

When I got back to the vicarage, Griselda met me in the hall. There were tears in her eyes. 'She's leaving.'

'Who's leaving?'

'Mary.'

'Well,' I said, 'we'll get another servant.'

'Len,' Griselda said. 'Don't you care?'

I didn't. In fact, I felt rather happy at the thought of no more burnt vegetables and tough meat.

'I suppose,' I said, 'that someone else has asked her to work for them.'

'No,' said Griselda. 'Nobody else wants her. But she's upset, so please go and talk to her.' And she pushed me into the kitchen before I could argue.

Mary was washing potatoes in the sink.

'Mrs Clement says that you wish to leave us,' I said. 'Will you tell me what has upset you?'

'I have never been in a house where they had a murder,' Mary said. 'And I never want to be again.'

'I think that is very unlikely,' I replied.

'Well, anyway, Colonel Protheroe sent lots of poor fellows to prison just for shooting at a bird. And then, before he's even been buried, his daughter comes here and says I don't do my work properly.'

'Do you mean that Miss Protheroe came to this house?'

'Yes. I found her here when I came back from that inquest. She was in the study. "I'm looking for my little yellow hat," she says. "I left it here the other day." "Well," I said, "There was no hat here when I cleaned the room on Thursday morning." And she said, "But I don't expect you would have seen it. You don't spend much time cleaning a room, do you?" And she pointed at some dust on the table. So I said, "If the vicar and his wife are satisfied, that is all that matters." And she laughed and said, "Oh! But are they?"'

'Mary,' I said. 'We would be very sorry to lose you.'

There were tears in Mary's eyes. 'I wouldn't like to upset you or Mrs Clement.'

'Then that's all right,' I said. I left the kitchen and found Griselda and Dennis waiting for me in the hall.

'She's staying,' I said, and told them what had upset Mary.

'How like Lettice,' said Dennis <u>lovingly</u>. 'She never knows where she's left anything. It's partly what makes her so attractive to everybody.'

'Not Lawrence Redding,' I said.

'Oh, but Lawrence is very attractive himself,' said Griselda. 'So he likes the quiet type. Like Anne. I don't think he has any idea that Lettice cares about him.'

'But she doesn't,' said Dennis. 'She doesn't even like him. She told me so.'

Griselda did not reply. She turned to me. 'I forgot to tell you, Len, Miss Marple has invited us over tonight after dinner, to entertain the nephew. I said we'd go.'

'Of course.'

I went into my study and walked over to the desk. Here Protheroe had sat when he had been shot. Here, where I was standing, his enemy had stood...

Then I noticed a flash of bright blue on the floor. I bent down. By the desk was a small object. I picked it up. It was a blue earring, and I remembered exactly where I had last seen it.

CHAPTER 21

Miss Marple's nephew, Raymond West, is supposed to be a wonderful writer. His books are about unpleasant people with very boring lives.

He turned immediately to Griselda and as they talked I heard her say, 'Do you have any ideas about the murder, Mr West?'

'Only that it is probably a very ordinary murder, by an angry poacher most likely.'

'Poor Mrs Protheroe,' Miss Marple said. 'There are so many letters to write. Miss Cram is going to Old Hall to help her. She is free this weekend because Dr Stone is not working on the barrow.'

'Stone?' said Raymond. 'Is that the archaeologist fellow?'

'Yes'

'I met him at a dinner not long ago and we had a most interesting talk. I must visit him.'

'He's just gone to London,' I said. 'In fact we bumped into you at the station this afternoon.'

'But that was a little fat man, with glasses. That wasn't Stone.'

'I don't understand,' I said.

'The suitcase, of course!' said Miss Marple. 'It reminds me of the man who went round the village pretending to be the Gas Inspector. He stole a lot of valuable things.'

'Now this really is interesting,' said Raymond West.

'But has it anything to do with the murder?' asked Griselda.

'It is,' Miss Marple said, 'another Strange Thing.'

'Yes,' I said. 'And I think the Inspector should be told about it.'

CHAPTER 22

Inspector Slack's orders, when I spoke to him on the telephone, were short and strong. We must say nothing to anybody about the suitcase. And a search for it would begin immediately.

Griselda and I returned home very excited. But soon Dennis followed me into my study, looking upset.

'What is the matter?' I asked

'I don't want to go into the Navy.'

I was very surprised. 'But you love the sea. That's the job you have always wanted to do.'

'I want to go into banking. I need to get rich quickly. You've got to be rich to marry a girl who expects to have everything she wants.'

'You know,' I said gently, 'not all girls are like Lettice Protheroe.'

He was suddenly angry. 'You don't like her. Nobody does. Even the Napiers are saying awful things about her! Just because she left their tennis party a bit early. But she was bored. And she's very kind really. I wanted to leave, too, but she said, no, because it would upset the Napiers. So I stayed. I would do anything for Lettice.'

Poor boy. We said goodnight and he went up to bed.

Next morning at breakfast Griselda showed me a note she had just received. It was from Anne Protheroe.

Dear Griselda,

Could you and the vicar come for lunch today? Something strange has happened, and I would like Mr Clement's advice.

With love,
Anne Protheroe.

'We must go, of course,' said Griselda. 'I wonder what has happened?'

'Well,' I said, 'the funeral is tomorrow morning. Perhaps it has something to do with that.'

At Old Hall we were shown into the sitting room. Miss Cram was there with Anne Protheroe.

'I saw a reporter at the inquest,' Anne said. 'He asked me if I wanted to find my husband's murderer, and I said, "Yes." And then he asked me whether I suspected anyone, and I said, "No." And then he said, did I think the person who committed the crime knew the village, and I said they certainly seemed to. And that was all. And now look at this!' She held out a newspaper.

Across the top were the words:

WIDOW SAYS SHE WILL NEVER REST TILL SHE HAS HUNTED DOWN HER HUSBAND'S MURDERER!

'It doesn't sound like me, does it?' said Anne.

Griselda and I agreed. We then went into the dining room for lunch, where Lettice joined us.

After we had had coffee, Anne said, 'I want to have a little talk with the vicar.'

I followed her up the stairs to her small sitting room. But to my surprise, she continued along to the end of the passage, then up some narrow stairs and into a large dark room under the roof. On the floor there were suitcases, broken furniture, and some pictures.

Anne smiled. 'I am sleeping very badly just now, and at about three o'clock this morning I thought I heard someone moving about the house. So I got up to find out. I thought that the sounds came from up above but when I called up these stairs, "Is anybody there?" there was no answer, so I went back to bed. Then today, I decided to come up here. And I found this!'

A picture was leaning against the wall with its back towards us. She turned it round. It was a picture of someone, but the face had been cut in such a violent way that it was <u>unrecognizable</u>.

'What a shocking thing,' I said. 'Who is the picture of?'

'I don't know. All these things were in the <u>attic</u> when I married Lucius and I've never looked at them before. Do you think I ought to tell the police about it?'

'I don't know. It doesn't seem to be connected with the murder. But it is another Strange Thing.'

I followed Anne down to her sitting room. 'What are your plans?' I asked suddenly.

'Oh, I'm going to live here for another six months! I don't want to. But I have to. Because otherwise people will say that I ran away – because I felt guilty. Especially when –' She paused. 'When the six months are over, I am going to marry Lawrence.'

'I thought', I said, 'that you would.'

She started to cry. 'You don't know how grateful I am to you. If we'd been planning to go away together, and then Lucius had died – it would be so awful now. But you made us both see how wrong it would be.'

'I, too, am grateful,' I said.

'But you know,' she sat up, 'unless the real murderer is found people will always think it was Lawrence. Especially when he marries me. That's another reason why I'm staying. I'm going to find out the truth, and that's why I asked Miss Cram to come here. I think she knows something and I want to watch her.'

'Then the very night she arrives, that picture is cut,' I said.

'You think she did it? But why?'

I couldn't think of an answer so I took the blue earring from my pocket. 'I believe this is yours.'

'Oh, yes!' She held out her hand. 'Where did you find it?'

But I did not put the jewel into her hand. 'Would you mind if I kept it a little longer?'

'Why, certainly.'

I then asked her about her financial situation. 'It is a rather rude question I know, but I am concerned.'

'I don't think it's rude at all. Lucius was very well off and he left things equally divided between me and Lettice. Old Hall goes to me, but Lettice can choose enough furniture for a small house, and she will have enough money to buy one.'

I said goodbye to Anne, but there was one more thing I needed to do. And when I found Lettice alone downstairs in the sitting room, I went in and shut the door.

'Lettice,' I said, and held out the earring, 'Why did you drop this in my study?'

'I never dropped anything in your study,' she said. 'And that's not mine. That's Anne's.'

'I know,' I said. 'But she has only been in my study once since the murder, and then she was dressed in black and did not wear blue earrings.'

'So, she must have dropped it before. She was wearing them on Thursday.'

'Thursday,' I said, 'was the day of the murder. Mrs Protheroe did come to the study, but only as far as the window, not inside the room.'

'Where did you find this?'

'Underneath the desk.'

'Then it looks,' said Lettice, 'as though she didn't speak the truth?'

'And now I know that you are not speaking the truth, Lettice. Because the last time I saw this earring was on Friday morning when I came to Old Hall with Colonel Melchett. It was lying with the other one in your stepmother's bedroom.'

'Oh—!' She burst into tears.

I said gently, 'Lettice, why did you do it?'

'What?' She jumped up, looking wild and frightened. 'What do you mean?'

'Was it because you disliked Anne?'

'Oh, yes!' She seemed suddenly confident again. 'So I put the thing under the desk. I hoped it would get her into trouble.'

I told her that I would return the earring to Anne and say nothing about how I had found it.

CHAPTER 23

Griselda and I went home separately as I wanted to go round by the barrow to see if the police had found the suitcase.

'Nothing yet, sir,' Hurst said. 'But this is the only place where Miss Cram could have hidden it. She was seen walking into the woods, and that path goes only to Old Hall, and to this barrow.'

I wished Hurst good luck and continued on towards the vicarage. I was almost there when an idea suddenly came into my brain. The day after the murder, I had found broken bushes beside the path. I had thought that Lawrence had broken them. But perhaps Dr Stone or Miss Cram had gone that way?

I had just reached the place so, once again, I pushed my way through the bushes. This time I noticed some more small branches were broken. Someone had been here since Lawrence and myself.

I soon came to the place where I had met Lawrence and continued on further. Suddenly it opened out into a little grassy space. There were trees above, but again there were some broken bushes. I went across and looked between them. And there, with great excitement, I saw something smooth hidden under the leaves. Then I pulled out a small suitcase. I tried to open it, but it was locked. As I stood up, I noticed a shiny brown stone lying on the ground. I picked it up and put it in my pocket. Then, carrying the suitcase, I continued on towards home.

When I reached the lane I immediately heard a familiar voice, 'Oh! Mr Clement. How clever of you! You've found it!'

'Yes, Miss Marple, I'm going to take it down to the police station.'

'You don't think it would be better to telephone?'

Of course it would be better to telephone. To walk through the village with the suitcase would only encourage gossip. So I went with Miss Marple into her house and telephoned Inspector Slack.

He arrived not long afterwards, and not in a good mood. 'Sir, if you thought you knew where this suitcase was hidden, why did you not tell the police?'

'Because I was in the woods when I suddenly thought about it.'

He had brought several keys with him and in one minute the suitcase was open. The first thing we saw was a red scarf. Next, there was a very old coat, then an old cap and an old pair of boots. At the bottom was a package wrapped in newspaper. The inspector tore it open.

For a moment no one spoke. Inside the parcel were some little silver objects and a silver plate.

'Colonel Protheroe's seventeenth century *tazza*!' Miss Marple cried.

'So that was their plan,' the inspector replied. 'Robbery. But no one has reported these things missing.'

'Perhaps they didn't know they were missing,' I suggested. 'Colonel Protheroe probably kept them locked away somewhere.'

'I must investigate this,' said the inspector. 'I'll go up to Old Hall now. That's why Dr Stone went to London. He was afraid that because of the murder we might search his rooms and find this silver. So he told the girl to put on these old clothes and go and hide the suitcase in the woods. Then, when it was safe, he planned to return and collect it one night. Well, this proves he had nothing to do with the murder.'

When he had gone, I said, 'Well, that's one mystery solved. And Stone is not a murder suspect.'

'It would seem so,' said Miss Marple. 'But isn't this silver very valuable?'

'A *tazza* sold the other day for over a thousand pounds.'

'That's what I mean. The sale would take some time to arrange. And a lot of people would know about it. But if the robbery was reported, well, the things couldn't be sold at all.'

'I don't quite understand.' I said.

'Well, it seems to me that the only way this silver could be sold would be if it had been replaced by copies. And of course, as you say, then Dr Stone would have no reason to murder Colonel Protheroe.'

'Exactly,' I said.

'Yes, but Colonel Protheroe did say that he was going to have all his things valued for insurance. He talked about it a lot. Of course, I don't know if he had made any actual arrangements, but if he had...'

'I see.'

'Of course, when the expert saw the silver, he would know it wasn't the real thing, and then Colonel Protheroe would remember that he had shown the things to Dr Stone...'

'I understand. And I think we ought to find out for certain.' I went once more to the telephone and called Old Hall. 'Mrs Protheroe, can you tell me if the contents of Old Hall were ever valued?'

Her answer came immediately. I thanked her, put down the telephone, and turned to Miss Marple. 'Colonel Protheroe had arranged for a man to come down from London on Monday – tomorrow – to make a full valuation. Because of the Colonel's death the arrangement was cancelled.'

'Then there was a reason for the murder,' said Miss Marple softly.

'A reason, yes, but when the shot was fired, Dr Stone was walking to the village with Mrs Protheroe and Lawrence Redding.'

'Yes,' said Miss Marple. 'So he can't have done it.'

CHAPTER 24

I returned to the vicarage and found my curate, Hawes, waiting for me in my study. He was walking up and down, and his whole body was shaking.

'My dear fellow,' I said. 'You really must go away for a rest.'

'Well, I did come to ask you if you would take the service tonight instead of me.'

'Of course. You are not well...'

'I am perfectly well. And I want to take the service. But I don't want all those eyes looking at me. And these pains in my head – could you give me a glass of water?'

I brought the water to him. Then he took a small box from his pocket, took a pill from the box, and swallowed it with the water.

'I hope you don't take too many of those,' I said.

'Oh, no. Dr Haydock warned me against that.' Then he looked over at the window. 'You have been up at Old Hall today, haven't you?'

'Yes.'

'Excuse me, but did Mrs Protheroe ask you to go there?'

I looked at him, surprised.

His face went red. 'I'm sorry. I just thought something had happened and that was why Mrs Protheroe had asked to see you.'

'She wanted to discuss the funeral arrangements.'

'Oh! That was all. I see.'

I did not reply.

Finally he said, 'Mr Redding came to see me last night. I don't know why.'

'Didn't he tell you?'

'He just said he was a bit lonely in the evenings. But what does he want to come and see me for? I don't like it! I never suggested that he was guilty. The only person I suspected was Archer.'

'Do you really think he shot Colonel Protheroe?' I asked.

'Colonel Protheroe sent him to prison. He was determined to punish him, so he had a lot to drink and then shot him. You must admit that's likely?'

'No, I don't.'

'Why not?'

'Because a man like Archer wouldn't kill a man with a pistol. It's the wrong weapon.'

Hawes looked shocked. It wasn't the answer he had expected. Soon he thanked me and left. I had gone to the front door with him, and on the hall table I saw four notes. They all looked as though they had been written by the same person, and they all said, *Urgent*. The only difference I could see was that one was much dirtier than the others.

Mary came out of the kitchen and saw me looking at them. 'They came by hand after lunch,' she said. 'All except one. I found that in the <u>letterbox</u>.'

I took them into the study. The first one said:

Dear Mr Clement,

I have heard something about the death of poor Colonel Protheroe. So I would like your advice about whether to go to the police or not. Perhaps you could come and see me this afternoon?

Yours sincerely,
Martha Price Ridley.

I opened the second:

Dear Mr Clement,

I am very worried. I have learned something that I think may be important. I am frightened of going to the police. Please, dear Vicar, could you come to my house this afternoon and help me?

Yours very sincerely,
Caroline Wetherby.

The third I could guess without reading it.

Dear Mr Clement,

I have heard something that is very important. I feel you should be the first to know about it. Will you call in and see me this afternoon?'

Amanda Hartnell.

I opened the fourth note.

Dear Vicar,

Your wife has been seen coming out of Mr Redding's cottage in a secretive manner. They are having a love affair. I think you ought to know.

A Friend.

I <u>crushed</u> the paper in my hand and threw it into the fire just as Griselda entered the room.

'What's that you're throwing away?' she asked.

'Rubbish,' I said. I took a box of matches from my pocket. But Griselda was too quick for me. She had picked up the paper and read it before I could stop her. Then she threw it back to me.

I lit it and watched it burn. Griselda had moved away. She was standing by the window looking out into the garden.

'Len,' she said.

'Yes, my dear.'

'When Lawrence came here, I told you that I had only known him slightly before. That wasn't true. I had known him rather well. In fact, I had been in love with him.'

'Why didn't you tell me?' I asked.

'Oh! Because you're so silly in some ways. Just because you're much older than I am, you think that I might like other men more than you.'

'You're very clever at hiding things,' I said.

'Yes. I rather enjoy it. But it was true that I didn't know about Lawrence and Anne. And I wondered why he hardly noticed me. I'm not used to it.' She paused. 'You do understand, Len?'

'Yes,' I said, 'I understand.'

But did I?

CHAPTER 25

I still felt upset about the <u>anonymous</u> letter. But I picked up the other three letters and left the vicarage.

I wondered what it was that the three ladies wanted to tell me. I also wondered whether Inspector Slack had returned from Old Hall, so I went to the police station and found that he had. And that Miss Cram had returned with him. She was sitting there and saying very loudly that she had never taken a suitcase to the woods.

'That awful old Miss Marple has made a mistake. And I am leaving right now. Unless you are going to arrest me.'

The Inspector answered by opening the door for her, and Miss Cram walked out.

'Well,' said Slack. 'Miss Marple may have made a mistake.'

'She may,' I said, 'but Miss Marple is usually right. What about the silver, Inspector?'

'It was all there at Old Hall. So one lot of silver must be a copy. There's a good man in Much Benham, who knows all about old silver and I've sent a car to fetch him. We'll soon know which is which. But robbery is unimportant compared with murder.'

I said goodbye and walked into the village to see the old ladies. I thought that, of course, the news they had heard must be the same thing. But I was wrong.

I went to Miss Hartnell's house first. 'So good of you to come. Nobody dislikes gossip more than I do, Vicar. But this is about duty.' I could see that she was enjoying herself. 'When I called on Mrs Lestrange on the afternoon of the murder I thought she was out. But I have heard that she has said she was at home all the time and that she didn't answer the door because – well, she didn't want to see me!'

'She has been ill,' I said.

'Ill? Nonsense. And it is not true that she was in the house. She wasn't. I know.'

'How can you possibly know?'

Miss Hartnell's face turned red. 'I had rung the bell twice. Perhaps three times. And I suddenly thought that perhaps it did not work.'

'Yes?' I knew that it was easy to hear the bell from outside.

'So I went round the house and knocked on the windows. And I looked through them as well, but there was no one in the house.'

'What time was this, Miss Hartnell?'

'It must have been nearly six o'clock. I went straight home afterwards, and Mrs Protheroe called at about half past six to borrow a gardening magazine. And all the time the poor colonel was lying murdered.'

'Is that all you wanted to tell me?'

'I thought it might be important, Mr Clement.'

I visited Miss Wetherby next. 'Dear Vicar, you are so kind to come round so quickly. You must understand that I heard this from someone who knows the truth.'

In St Mary Mead a person who knows the truth is always someone else's servant. 'So, who was that?'

'I promised that I would tell no one their name. And I always keep a promise. Well, this person said they saw a certain lady walk up the road that goes to the vicarage. But before that, this lady looked around in a very strange way, to see if anyone had noticed her. This was just before six o'clock.'

'On which day?'

Miss Wetherby gave a little cry 'The day of the murder, of course!'

'And the name of the lady?'

'Begins with an L,' said Miss Wetherby.

There was still Mrs Price Ridley to see. And the first thing she said was, 'I will not say anything at all to the police. But I have heard of something that I think they should know about.'

'Does it involve Mrs Lestrange?' I asked.

'Why should it?'

I said no more.

'It is very simple,' she continued. 'My servant, Clara, was standing at the front gate, when she heard a sneeze.'

'Yes?'

'That's all. She heard a sneeze.'

'But,' I said, 'why is that strange?'

Mrs Price Ridley said very slowly, 'She heard a sneeze on the day of the murder at a time when there was no one in your house. Because the murderer was hiding in the bushes. What you have to look for is a man with a bad cold.'

'Well, our servant, Mary, has a bad cold. It must have been her sneeze Clara heard.'

'It was a man's sneeze,' said Mrs Price Ridley. 'And Clara couldn't hear Mary sneeze in your kitchen if she was standing at my gate.'

'You couldn't hear anyone sneezing in my study from your gate,' I said.

'But the man might have been hiding in the bushes,' said Mrs Price Ridley. 'Well, that is all I have to say.'

I said goodbye, and as I left, I asked Clara about the sneeze.

'It's quite true, sir, I heard a sneeze. And it wasn't an ordinary sneeze.'

Nothing about a crime is ever ordinary. The sneeze was, I imagined, a special murderer's sneeze. I decided to visit Dr Haydock and went down the road to his house.

'How good to see you,' he said. 'What's the news?'

I told him about Stone.

'Well, that explains a lot. He had read about archaeology, but he kept making mistakes and Protheroe must have noticed. You remember the disagreement they had. What about Miss Cram? Is she involved?'

'The police aren't sure.' I then told him that I was worried about my curate, Hawes, and that I was anxious that he should get away for a rest.

'Yes. I suppose that would be the best thing. Poor fellow.'

'I thought you didn't like him.'

'I don't. But I'm sorry for a lot of people I don't like. I'm even sorry for Protheroe. Nobody ever liked him because he always thought he was right, and that others were always wrong. He was the same even when he was a young man.'

'So, you knew him then?'

'Oh, yes! When we lived in Westmorland, I had a surgery not far from his house. But that was twenty years ago. Is that all you came to tell me, Clement?' Dr Haydock was watching me. So I told him about my talks with Miss Hartnell and Miss Wetherby. He paused, then said, 'It's true. I've been trying to protect Mrs Lestrange from anything that might upset her. She's an old friend, but that's not my only reason. Mrs Lestrange is dying.'

'What?'

'She has about a month to live. And on the evening of the murder she was here, in this house.'

'But she wasn't here when I sent Mary for you. I mean, when we discovered the body.'

'No. She'd gone to meet someone.'

'In her own house?'

'I don't know, Clement.'

I believed him but I suspected that he knew more than he said. Then I thought of something, and I took from my pocket the shiny brown stone I had found in the woods. I held it out to him and asked him what it was.

'Looks like <u>picric acid</u>.'

'What is picric acid?'

'It's an <u>explosive</u>. Where did you find it?

I shook my head. He had his secrets. Well, I would have mine.

CHAPTER 26

That evening, as I sat down to dinner, Griselda said, 'Oh, I forgot to tell you, Len, this note arrived for you when you were out.'

I took it and shook my head. Across the top was written: *By hand – Urgent.*

'This', I said, 'must be from Miss Marple. She's the only old lady who hasn't written to me today.' I was right.

Dear Mr Clement,

I would very much like to talk to you. I will come over at half past nine. Perhaps dear Griselda and Dennis would be very kind and come over here and entertain my nephew. If I do not hear, I will come at the time I have said.

Yours very sincerely,
Jane Marple.

I handed the note to Griselda.

'Oh, we'll go!' she said cheerfully.

They left at just after nine o'clock, and at half past nine exactly, there was a little knock on my study window, and I opened the glass door for Miss Marple to come in.

'I think that you are wondering why I am so interested in this murder. I would like to explain.' She paused, and I offered her a chair. 'You see, because I live alone, I need a hobby. I could, of course, choose sewing or drawing, but my hobby is Human Nature. It is so interesting. And when there is a mystery and I think I know the answer, it is so satisfying to find that I am right.'

'You usually are,' I said, smiling. Then I told her about the three notes I had received that afternoon. I told her about the picture at Old Hall with the person's face cut. I told her how Miss Cram had behaved at the police station. And I also told her about the shiny brown stone I had found. 'But it's probably got nothing to do with the case,' I continued. 'Dr Haydock said it was picric acid.' I then asked her the question that I had wanted to ask her for some time. 'Miss Marple, who do you suspect? You said that there were seven people.'

'At least, yes,' said Miss Marple. 'But the point is, that each thing has got to be explained correctly. And that's very difficult. If it wasn't for that note...'

'The note?'

'Yes, that note is wrong, somehow.'

'But,' I said, 'it has been explained. It was written at six thirty-five and another person – the murderer – put the incorrect time 6.20 at the top.'

'But even so,' said Miss Marple, 'it's all wrong.'

'But why?'

'Listen.' She leaned forward excitedly. 'Mrs Protheroe walked past my garden, and she went to the study window and she looked in and she didn't see Colonel Protheroe.'

'Because he was writing at the desk,' I said.

'And that's what's all wrong. That was at twenty past six. He wouldn't have needed to tell you that he couldn't wait any longer until after half past six. So, why was he sitting at the desk then?'

'I never thought of that,' I said.

'Let us think about it again. Mrs Protheroe went to the window and thought the study was empty. Otherwise she would not have gone down to the studio to meet Mr Redding. And that leaves three possibilities.'

'Does it?'

'The first is that Colonel Protheroe was dead already, but I don't think that's likely. He'd only been there for five minutes. The second possibility is, of course, that he was sitting at the desk writing a note, but it must have been a different note from the one that was found. And the third...'

'Yes?' I said.

'Well, the third is, of course, that the room really was empty.'

'You mean that after he had been shown in, he went out again and came back later?'

'Yes.'

'But why would he have done that?'

Miss Marple shook her head and stood up. 'I must go home. It has been good to have this little talk.'

'Thank you,' I said. 'But I feel more confused than before.'

'Oh! Don't say that. I have one idea that fits nearly everything. That is, except for one coincidence. And I think one coincidence is all right. More than one, of course, is not.'

'So you really think that you know who killed Colonel Protheroe?' I asked.

'Yes, except for... If only that note had said something different.' She moved towards the window and on her way put her hand into the pot of a rather tired house plant. 'Poor thing. Your servant should water this plant every day. I suppose it is Mary who looks after it?'

'I'm not sure that "looks after" are the right words for anything that Mary does,' I said. 'She came back from the inquest and found Lettice Protheroe here. And Lettice told her that she didn't clean properly. It upset her.'

'Oh!' Miss Marple was just about to step into the garden when she suddenly stopped. 'So that was it! Perfectly possible all the time.' She turned to me. 'I have been stupid – very, very stupid. Goodnight, Mr Clement.' And she went quickly across the grass towards her house.

Chapter 27

I had just sat down at my desk again, when the doorbell rang. I went to answer it and saw there was a letter in the letterbox. I took it out, but as I did so the bell rang again, so I put the letter in my pocket and opened the front door.

It was Colonel Melchett. 'Hello, Clement. I'm on my way home from town. Thought I'd just say hello and see if you could give me a drink.'

'I'd be happy to. Come into the study.'

Melchett followed me there and I went and got a bottle of wine and two glasses.

'I've got one bit of news for you, Clement. You know that letter that Protheroe was writing when he was killed?'

'Yes.'

'We got an expert to look at it – to say whether the 6.20 was written by someone else. And, of course, we sent him examples of Protheroe's writing. And do you know the result? That letter was never written by Protheroe at all. They still think the 6.20 was written by someone else – but they're not sure.'

'Really? Miss Marple said this evening that the note was all wrong.'

We looked at each other. Then the telephone rang. I went over and answered it.

'I want to confess,' a high, nervous voice screamed at me. 'I want to confess!'

Then the line went dead. I put the phone down, and turned to Melchett. 'You once said that you would go mad if anyone else confessed to the crime.'

'Yes?'

'That was someone who wanted to confess, and we were cut off.'

Melchett rushed to the telephone. 'I'll speak to the operator.'

'Do,' I said. 'I'm going out. I think I recognized that voice.'

CHAPTER 28

I hurried down the village street. It was eleven o'clock at night, but when I saw a light in a certain upstairs window, I stopped and rang the door bell. There was the sound of feet, then a key turned in the lock, and a woman opened the door.

'Why, it's the vicar!' she said.

'Good evening, Mrs Sadler,' I replied. 'I am sorry it's so late. But I want to see your <u>lodger</u>, Mr Hawes.' I went quickly up the stairs. Hawes was asleep in a chair. An empty pill bottle and a glass of water were on a table beside him. On the floor, was a letter. I picked it up.

It began, *My dear Clement.*

I read it all, then picked up the telephone and asked the operator for the vicarage. They told me the line was busy. So I asked them to call me when the line was free.

I then took out of my pocket the note that I had found in the vicarage letterbox. The writing was the same as that on the other anonymous letter that I received earlier. I tore it open. I read it once – twice – but I still could not believe what it said.

I was beginning to read it a third time when the telephone rang. Like a man in a dream, I picked it up.

'Melchett here. Where are you? I've found out about that call. The number is—'

'I know the number.'

'Is that where you are speaking from?'

'Yes.'

'So you've got the murderer?'

'I don't know,' I said. 'You'd better come here.' I gave him the address. Then I sat down and read the anonymous letter again.

CHAPTER 29

It felt as though years had passed when I heard the door open and Melchett entered the room. He saw Hawes asleep in his chair. 'What's happened, Clement?'

I passed him one of the letters and he read it aloud.

My dear Vicar,

It is a very unpleasant thing that I have to tell you. But I know who is guilty of the crime. It is very painful for me to name a priest of your church. But it is my duty and...

Here the writing ended. Melchett looked at Hawes. 'So it's the one man we never even thought about!' He went over to the sleeping man and shook him, at first gently, then harder. 'He's not asleep! He's drugged!' He picked up the pill box. 'Has he...?'

'I think so,' I said. 'It's his way out, poor fellow.'

But Melchett had caught a murderer and he wanted his murderer punished. He picked up the telephone and asked for Dr Haydock's number.

'Hello – hello – hello – Will the doctor come round at once to see Mr Hawes. It's urgent... What?... Well, what number is it, then?... Oh, sorry.' He rang off. 'Wrong number! HELLO, you gave me the wrong number... Yes, give me three nine – nine, not five.' And then, 'Hello – is that you, Haydock? Melchett speaking. Come to see Hawes at once, will you? At once, I say!' He put the phone down and turned to me. 'Where did you find this letter, Clement?'

'On the floor – where it had fallen from his hand.'

'So Miss Marple was right about us finding the wrong note. But why didn't the stupid fellow destroy this one? It just proves he's guilty! Listen, that sounds like a car.' He went to the window. 'Yes, it's Haydock all right.'

A moment later the doctor entered the room. He went across to Hawes and quickly examined him. 'I'm not sure that I can save him, Melchett.'

'Do everything possible.'

'Right. Well, I must drive him to the hospital at Much Benham. Help me to carry him down to the car.'

We both did so. As Dr Haydock climbed into the driving seat, he said, 'You won't be able to put him in prison. The poor fellow wasn't responsible for his actions. And I shall give evidence for him.'

'What did he mean by that?' asked Melchett as we went upstairs again.

I explained that Hawes had been ill with sleeping sickness.

'Always some good reason nowadays for every dirty action, isn't there?'

But before I could disagree there was an interruption. The door opened and Miss Marple walked in. 'So sorry, Colonel Melchett, but when I heard that Mr Hawes was ill, I felt I must come and see if I could do something.'

'Very kind of you, Miss Marple,' Melchett said. 'But how did you know Hawes was ill?'

'The telephone. You thought you were speaking to Dr Haydock. But you were speaking to me. My number is three five.'

'Well, anyway, there is nothing you can do,' Melchett said. 'Because Haydock has taken Hawes to hospital.'

'Oh, that is good news! He will be safe there.' She was looking at the pill box. 'I suppose he took too many of those?'

'I think you should read this,' I said, and gave her Protheroe's unfinished letter. She took it and read it. 'Mr Clement, why did you come here this evening?'

I explained about the telephone call and how I had thought I recognized Hawes' voice. Miss Marple nodded. 'So you got here just in time.'

'Don't you think,' I said, 'that it might be better if Hawes didn't recover? We know the truth now and...'

'Of course,' Miss Marple said. 'Of course! That's what he wants you to think! That you know the truth – and that it's best for everyone as it is. Oh, yes, it all fits in – the letter, and the pills, and poor Mr Hawes' confession. But it's all wrong. That's why I am so glad Mr Hawes is safe in hospital where no one can reach him. If he gets better, he will tell you the truth.'

'The truth?'

'Yes – that he never killed Colonel Protheroe.'

'But the telephone call,' I said. 'The letter – the pills. It's all so clear.'

'That's what he wants you to think. Oh, he's very clever! Keeping the letter and using it this way was very clever indeed.'

'Who do you mean', I said, 'by "he"?'

'I mean the murderer,' said Miss Marple. 'I mean Mr Lawrence Redding...'

We looked at her and said nothing. I really think that for a moment we thought she had gone mad. Colonel Melchett was the first to speak. 'That is nonsense, Miss Marple. Mr Redding has been proved to be innocent.'

'Of course,' said Miss Marple. 'He made sure of that.'

'No,' said Colonel Melchett. 'He did his best to get himself arrested for the murder.'

'Yes,' said Miss Marple. 'He led us all in that direction, including me. You remember, Mr Clement, that I was quite shocked when I heard Mr Redding had confessed to the crime. It upset all my ideas and made me think he was not guilty – when up to then I had been sure that he was.'

'So it was Lawrence Redding you suspected?' I asked.

'I know that in books it is always the most unlikely person. But in real life it is usually the most obvious one. I have always liked Mrs Protheroe but I soon realized that she would do anything Lawrence Redding told her. And, of course, he is not the sort of young man who would marry a woman who has no money. So first it was necessary for Colonel Protheroe to be removed.'

'Absolute nonsense!' Colonel Melchett cried. 'We know everything that Redding was doing up to 6.50 and Dr Haydock says Protheroe could not have been shot then.'

'No indeed. Because it was Mrs Protheroe who shot Colonel Protheroe – not Mr Redding.'

Again we looked at her.

'I did not think it was right to speak until now, because I still needed one more fact in order to explain what had happened. Then suddenly, just as I was leaving Mr Clement's study, I noticed the plant in the pot by the window – and – well, there it was! Clear as day!'

'Mad – quite mad,' Melchett whispered to me.

But Miss Marple just smiled and continued, 'I liked Anne and Lawrence, so when they both confessed in that silly way – well, I was happy that I had been wrong. And I began to think of other people who might want Colonel Protheroe dead.'

'The seven suspects,' I said quietly.

'Yes, indeed. There was Archer. And there was your Mary. She's been Archer's girlfriend for a long time, and she was alone in the house when it happened! And then, of course, there was Lettice – wanting freedom and money to do as she liked. And Dennis, who would do anything for Lettice.'

'No!' I cried.

'And then, of course, there is poor Mr Hawes. And you.'

'Me?' I said.

'Well, yes. There was that church money that disappeared. Either you or Mr Hawes must have taken it. Of course, I was always sure it was Mr Hawes, but then... there was also dear Griselda.'

'But Mrs Clement was not even here,' interrupted Melchett. 'She returned from London on the 6.50 train.'

'That's what she told you,' said Miss Marple. 'But that train was half an hour late. And at a quarter past seven I saw her walking to Old Hall. So she must have come back on an earlier train.' She looked at me. 'In fact she was seen. But perhaps you know that?'

I gave her the second anonymous letter I had received. It said that Griselda had been seen leaving Lawrence Redding's cottage at twenty past six on the day of the murder. It had made me think about the past romance between Lawrence and Griselda.

Perhaps Protheroe had found out about it and was going to tell me. So Griselda stole the pistol and shot him before I got home.

Miss Marple handed me back the note. 'But by Thursday afternoon the crime had been very carefully planned. Lawrence Redding first called on the vicar, knowing that he was out. He had with him the pistol which he hid in that plant pot. When the vicar came in, Lawrence explained that he had called to tell him that he had decided to leave the village. At five-thirty, he telephoned the vicar from the North Lodge, pretending he was the wife of a dying man.

'Mrs Protheroe and her husband had just gone into the village. And, very strangely, she did not take her handbag. Just before twenty past six she walked past my garden and stopped to speak to me. This was so that I would notice that she had no gun with her. Then she went round the corner of the house to the study window. The poor colonel was sitting at the desk writing his letter to you. She took the pistol from the pot, came up behind him and shot him. Then she dropped the pistol on the floor and walked down to the studio!'

'But the shot?' said Melchett. 'You didn't hear the shot?'

'There is, I think, something called a Maxim silencer. So perhaps the sneeze that Mrs Price Ridley's servant heard might have been the shot? But anyway, Mrs Protheroe and Mr Redding went into the studio together – and then realized, of course, that I would not leave my garden until I saw them come out again!'

I smiled at Miss Marple's <u>humorous</u> understanding of her own character.

'But when they did come out, their behaviour was happy and normal. And that was a bad mistake. Because if they had really said goodbye to each other they would have been sad. But because of the murder they did not dare to appear upset. For the next ten minutes they were careful to be seen by people in the village, then at last Mr Redding went back to the vicarage. He picked up the pistol and the silencer, and left the <u>forged</u> letter with the time written on it in blue ink. But when he left the letter, he found the one written by Colonel Protheroe. And he thought that it might be useful, so he put it in his pocket.

'Then he altered the time of the clock to the same as on the forged letter. He did not know that it was always kept a quarter of an hour ahead. He did this to make it seem that someone was trying to make Mrs Protheroe look guilty. Then he left the vicarage, and met you outside, Vicar. And he acted as though he was very upset. Which was clever. Because someone who had just committed a murder would, of course, try to behave normally. Then he got rid of the silencer and strode into the police station with the pistol and confessed to the crime.'

'What about the shot heard in the woods?' I asked. 'Was that the coincidence you mentioned?'

'Oh, no!' Miss Marple shook her head. 'It was absolutely necessary for a shot to be heard because without it Mrs Protheroe might have continued to be a suspect. I believe that picric acid explodes if you drop something heavy onto it. And remember, Vicar, that you met Mr Redding carrying a large stone in that same place in the woods where you found the picric acid later.'

'But the shot was heard at 6.30 when Lawrence and Anne had come out of the studio. You saw them.'

'Mr Redding had probably used some rope to hang the stone above the picric acid. Then he set fire to the end of the rope, knowing that it would take about twenty minutes to burn through and for the stone to fall and cause the explosion. When you met him, he had just picked up the stone to take it away.'

'So that no one could discover what had happened?'

'Yes, but when you appeared, he pretended that he was bringing it to me for my Japanese garden. Only...' Miss Marple paused. 'It was the wrong sort of stone for my garden! And that made me think.'

'But what about Hawes?' Melchett said. 'He has confessed to the crime.'

'Yes, but a different one. Poor Mr Hawes felt more and more guilty about taking the money from the collection.'

'What?'

'As I said, Mr Redding kept Colonel Protheroe's letter, and he realized that the Colonel was saying that Mr Hawes was the thief. So he came back here with Mr Hawes last night and, I think, managed to put some much stronger pills in Mr Hawes' box. Then, when Mr Hawes was unconscious, he put this letter into his pocket. When the poor young man was found dead and the letter was read, everyone would think that he had shot Colonel Protheroe and killed himself because he felt so guilty. In fact I think that Mr Hawes must have found that letter tonight. And, in his confused state, he decided to confess.'

'But what about the other telephone call?' Colonel Melchett asked. 'The one from Mr Redding's cottage to Mrs Price Ridley?'

'Ah!' said Miss Marple. 'That *is* the coincidence. Dear Griselda made that call. She and Dennis had heard that Mrs Price Ridley had been gossiping about the vicar and the church money. And they thought that this would make her stop. The coincidence was that the call was made at exactly the same time as the pretend shot from the wood. So it seemed that the two must be connected.'

'Your explanation is a very good one, Miss Marple,' Melchett said. 'But I don't believe you can prove any of it.'

'I know,' said Miss Marple. 'But you do believe it is true, don't you?'

'Yes, I do. But we need the proof!'

Miss Marple coughed. 'That is why I thought perhaps —'

'Yes?'

'We might be allowed to set a little <u>trap</u>.'

CHAPTER 31

I looked at her, shocked. 'A trap? What kind of a trap?'

'What if someone telephoned Mr Redding and warned him,' Miss Marple said. 'Suppose Dr Haydock mentioned that Mrs Sadler had seen him changing the pills in Mr Hawes' box – well, if Mr Redding is innocent, that would mean nothing to him. But if he isn't...'

'He might do something stupid,' I said.

'And prove he's guilty,' said Melchett. 'Yes, but would Haydock be willing to do that?'

Miss Marple interrupted him excitedly. 'Oh, it was just a thought. But here is Dr Haydock, so we can ask him.'

Haydock came into the room, looking very tired. 'I think Hawes is going to live. Although perhaps I wish that he wasn't.'

'You may think differently,' said Melchett, 'when you have heard what we now know.' And he quickly told him about Miss Marple's explanation of the crime. And then he told him of her idea.

Haydock's gentle opinions about criminals changed immediately. 'If this is true,' he said. 'I'll do anything you want. That poor fellow Hawes, he nearly died. And if he hadn't, he would have been found guilty of murder. Lawrence Redding deserves the heaviest punishment possible.' So he began to arrange the trap with Melchett. And I walked Miss Marple home.

CHAPTER 32

There is not much more to tell. Miss Marple's plan succeeded. Lawrence Redding was not an innocent man, and so the news that Mrs Sadler had seen him change Mr Hawes' pills did indeed make him do 'something stupid'.

His first thought, I imagine, must have been to run away. But he could not leave without telling Anne. So he went up to Old Hall that night – and two of Colonel Melchett's policemen followed him. He threw small stones at Anne's window to wake her up and she came down to the garden to talk to him. So the two policemen heard the whole conversation. And it proved that Miss Marple had been right in every detail.

Lawrence Redding and Anne Protheroe were accused of the murder and found guilty in court. Inspector Slack was praised for his energy and ability. Nothing at all was said about Miss Marple's part in solving the crime. And that was how she wanted it.

Lettice came to see me just after they were arrested. She wandered into my study and told me that she had always been sure her stepmother was involved. Saying that she had lost her yellow hat had been an excuse to search my study. She hoped that she would find something the police had not. But when she had found nothing, she had dropped Anne's earring by the desk.

'I knew she had done it, so what did it matter if that proved she had killed him?'

There are some things that Lettice will never understand.

'What are you going to do now?' I asked her.

'When it's all over, I am going abroad. With my mother.'

I looked up, surprised.

'Didn't you guess? Mrs Lestrange is my mother. She is dying, and she wanted to see me, so she came down here using a different name. Dr Haydock helped her. He was in love with her once. I think he still is. Anyway, she went to see father and told him she was dying and wanted to see me so much. Father was an awful man. He said "I thought she was dead!"'

'But mother sent a note to me, and I arranged to leave the tennis party early and meet her near the vicarage at a quarter past six. We left each other before half past six. But afterwards I was frightened that the police might think she had killed father. That was why I cut up that old picture of her. I was afraid the police might recognize it. Dr Haydock was frightened, too. Sometimes, I believe, he really thought she had done it!' She paused. 'It's strange. She and I belong to each other. Father and I didn't. But mother – well, I shall be with her till the end...' She got up and I held her hand. 'Some day, I hope, you will be happy. You deserve it, Lettice.'

'Do I really?' she said, with a little laugh. 'I'm not sure about that. Goodbye, Mr Clement. You've been very kind to me always – you and Griselda.'

Griselda!

I needed to tell her how badly the anonymous letter had upset me. At first she laughed. And then she told me that I should have trusted her.

'However,' she added, 'I'm going to be very serious and well behaved from now on.'

I found it hard to imagine Griselda like that.

She continued, 'You see, Len, I have something new coming into my life. It's coming into your life, too! And you can't call me a dear child any more when we have a real child of our own. I have also decided that since now I'm going to be a real "wife and mother" I must look after the house as well. So I have bought two books: one on House Management and one on Mother Love.'

'You haven't bought a book on How to Treat a Husband, have you?' I asked, as I put my arms round her.

'I don't need to,' said Griselda. 'I love you so much. What more do you want?'

'Nothing,' I said.

'Could you say, just once, that you love me madly?'

'Griselda,' I said, 'Not only that, but I <u>worship</u> you!'

My wife was just about to kiss me when suddenly she pulled away.

'Miss Marple's coming. Don't say a word to her about the baby. I don't want everyone telling me to lie down all the time. Tell her I've gone to play tennis. That will stop her thinking anything about babies.'

Miss Marple came to the window, smiled, and asked for Griselda.

'Griselda', I said, 'has gone to play tennis.'

'Oh, but surely...' There was a worried expression in Miss Marple's eyes. 'That is not wise just now.' And then her face went pink.

So we quickly started to talk about the Protheroe case, and of 'Dr Stone', who had turned out to be a well-known thief. Miss Cram, though, had been cleared of any crime. She had at last told the police that she had taken the suitcase to the woods, but had thought she was protecting Dr Stone's archaeological discoveries from his enemies.

Then Miss Marple said, 'I hope dear Griselda is not doing too much. I was in the bookshop in Much Benham yesterday...'

Poor Griselda – that book on Mother Love had given Miss Marple the clue!

'I wonder,' I said, 'if you were to commit a murder whether you would ever be found out.'

'What an awful idea,' said Miss Marple. 'And how naughty of you, Mr Clement.' She got up. 'But of course you are feeling very cheerful.' She paused by the window. 'My love to dear Griselda – and tell her that any little secret is safe with me.'

Really Miss Marple is rather sweet...

◆ Character List ◆

The Rev Leonard (Len) Clement: the vicar of St Mary Meade

Griselda Clement: the vicar's wife

Dennis: the vicar's nephew

Mary: the servant at the vicarage

Mr Hawes: the vicar's curate

Miss Jane Marple: a very observant elderly lady living near the vicarage

Mrs Price Ridley: an elderly lady

Miss Wetherby: an elderly unmarried lady

Miss Hartnell: an elderly unmarried lady

Colonel Protheroe: a wealthy man, and churchwarden

Anne Protheroe: Colonel Protheroe's wife

Lettice Protheroe: Colonel Protheroe's daughter from his first marriage

Mrs Lestrange: a beautiful older woman, new to the village

Lawrence Redding: a handsome young artist

Dr Stone: an archaeologist – visiting the village to examine an old burial ground on the Colonel's land

Miss Cram: Dr Stone's secretary

Dr Haydock: the village doctor

Inspector Slack: the policeman in charge of the murder case

Constable Hurst: a policeman dealing with the murder case

Colonel Melchett: the Chief Constable dealing with the murder case

Raymond West: Miss Marple's nephew, a writer

Rose: a servant at Colonel Protheroe's house

Gladdie: a servant at Colonel Protheroe's house

Archer: a poacher and Mary's boyfriend

Mrs Archer: Archer's mother, and cleaner for Lawrence Redding

Clara: servant to Mrs Price Ridley

◆ Cultural notes ◆

1. The Church of England
Many English villages have a church belonging to the Church of England.

The administrative area of the church and the surrounding villages is called a parish. Each parish is looked after by a vicar – the name for a priest in the Church of England. The vicar is paid by the church and lives in a house called a vicarage. This belongs to the church. Vicars in the Church of England are allowed to marry.

The vicar leads church services, during which he gives a sermon – a talk about spiritual and religious matters. The vicar is responsible for taking care of the spiritual needs of the people of the village, so often visits those who are ill or have other worries. The vicar will carry out baptisms, marriage ceremonies and funerals and is generally a very respected person in the local area. People will often ask the vicar for advice regarding personal matters. In the story, the vicar, Leonard Clement, often has to visit local people to help solve their problems, or to support relatives when illness or death occurs. He would also be asked to advise on other personal or moral problems.

The vicar is sometimes assisted by a curate, who is a less experienced priest – in the story this is Mr Hawes. The vicar is also helped by people in the parish called churchwardens – Colonel Protheroe is one of them. Churchwardens are not paid but give their time to support the vicar with practical matters, such as handling the church's money and maintaining the church buildings.

The people of the village help the church to do its work by putting money in a collection bag, which is passed around those attending church services. The story begins with a dispute about a £1 note that has gone missing. One pound in those days was a considerable sum of money – approximately 50 pounds today.

2. Village life

An English village is a small group of houses in the countryside, usually with a church at its centre. Sometimes there is a very large house in a village where rich people live. They may own the local farm land and the houses of farm workers. This is the case with Colonel Protheroe, who owns the house called *Old Hall*. A village often has a post office, an inn (or pub), and a shop. It may also have a local doctor.

Historically, village life was quieter and slower than life in a town and everyone knew who everyone else was, even if they did not meet socially. They also knew quite a lot about each other's lives. In this story there is much discussion amongst the characters about the personal lives of certain individuals. This gossip meant rumours circulated quickly round a small village.

At the time that this story was written, village life was very traditional and conservative. Few people had cars, so ordinary village people led quite isolated lives, especially if they were far from large towns or cities. The train was the only means of long distance transport for most people.

3. Archaeology

This is the study of our human past. Archaeologists dig up and examine the remains of things that have been left by people in the past. These are usually the remains of buildings, tools, weapons and cooking utensils. In the story, the archaeologist, Dr Stone, is investigating an ancient place called a barrow where important people were buried in the distant past.

4. The structure of the police in England

The structure of the police force and the ranks of the men and women who work there have not changed much since the Metropolitan Police was created in London in 1829. The ranks, starting at the lowest, are:

Police Constable, Sergeant, Inspector, Chief Inspector, Superintendent, Chief Superintendent.

Throughout the country there is a structure of separate but co-operating police forces. Each one has a Chief Constable in charge. The Chief Constable does not usually participate in police operations but is more of a manager who makes important decisions. In this story, however, the Chief Constable, Colonel Melchett, becomes actively involved in the case, because the victim, Colonel Protheroe, was a very important person in the village.

5. Telephone system
At the time of the story, telephone calls were handled by an operator at the local telephone exchange. The operator would physically connect the caller to the number required. In the case of the village in the story, and because only a relative few people had telephones, it would be easy for Inspector Slack to identify who called who at any particular time, and where the call came from.

6. Inquest
In cases of sudden, violent or suspicious death, it is common to hold a public inquiry called an inquest to find out why the person died. The coroner is the person in charge of the inquest, and the official cause of death is decided by a jury of twelve ordinary people chosen from the local community.

At the inquest the coroner and the jury hears medical evidence, as well as evidence from any other people that may be relevant. The family of the person who died, and members of the public can also attend the inquest.

Once all the evidence has been heard, the jury gives its verdict – for example natural death (i.e. a heart attack), accidental death, suicide or murder.

✦ GLOSSARY ✦

adore TRANSITIVE VERB
If you **adore** someone, you feel great love and admiration for them.

alibi COUNTABLE NOUN
If you have an **alibi**, you can prove that you were somewhere else when a crime was committed.

anonymous ADJECTIVE
Something that is **anonymous** does not reveal who you are.

archaeologist COUNTABLE NOUN
An **archaeologist** studies societies and peoples of the past by examining the remains of their buildings, tools, and other objects.

attic COUNTABLE NOUN
An **attic** is a room at the top of a house just below the roof.

avenger COUNTABLE NOUN
An **avenger** is someone who hurts or punishes a person who is responsible for a wrong or harmful act.

barrow COUNTABLE NOUN
A **barrow** is a large structure made of earth that people used to build over graves in ancient times.

bathing dress COUNTABLE NOUN
A **bathing dress** is a piece of clothing which women wear when they go swimming.

blackmail TRANSITIVE VERB
If one person **blackmails** another person, they threaten to reveal a secret about them, unless they do something they are told to do, such as giving money.

bump into PHRASAL VERB
If you **bump into** someone you know, you meet them unexpectedly.

burial ground COUNTABLE NOUN
A **burial ground** is a place where bodies are buried, especially an ancient place.

Chief Constable COUNTABLE NOUN
A **Chief Constable** is the officer who is in charge of the police force in a particular county or area in Britain.

churchwarden COUNTABLE NOUN
In the Anglican Church, a **churchwarden** is the person who has been chosen by a congregation to help the vicar of a parish with administration and other duties.

collection bag COUNTABLE NOUN
A **collection bag** is a bag that is used to collect money for charity.

colonel TITLE NOUN
A **colonel** is a senior officer in an army, air force, or the marines.

congeal INTRANSITIVE VERB
When a liquid **congeals**, it becomes very thick and sticky and almost solid.

constable COUNTABLE NOUN
In Britain and some other countries, a **constable** is a police officer of the lowest rank.

coroner COUNTABLE NOUN
A **coroner** is an official who is responsible for investigating the deaths of people who have died in a sudden, violent, or unusual way.

crush TRANSITIVE VERB
To **crush** something means to press it very hard so that its shape is destroyed or so that it breaks into pieces.

curate COUNTABLE NOUN
A **curate** is a clergyman in the Anglican Church who helps the priest.

dining room COUNTABLE NOUN
The **dining room** is the room in a house where people have their meals, or a room in a hotel where meals are served.

dreamy ADJECTIVE
If you describe a person as **dreamy**, you mean that they are not very practical.

drip INTRANSITIVE VERB
When liquid **drips** somewhere, it falls in individual small drops.

explosive VARIABLE NOUN
An **explosive** is a substance or device that can cause an explosion.

fellow COUNTABLE NOUN
A **fellow** is an old-fashioned word for a man or boy.

fingerprint COUNTABLE NOUN
Fingerprints are marks made by a person's fingers which show the lines on the skin. Everyone's fingerprints are different, so they can be used to identify criminals.

footprint COUNTABLE NOUN
A **footprint** is a mark in the shape of a foot that a person or animal makes in or on a surface.

forged ADJECTIVE
If something such as a banknote, letter, or painting is **forged**, it has been copied to make it so that it looks genuine, in order to deceive people.

forgiveness UNCOUNTABLE NOUN
If you believe in **forgiveness**, you believe that people should be forgiven for something wrong that they have done.

for someone's sake PHRASE
When you do something **for someone's sake**, you do it in order to help them or make them happy.

frown INTRANSITIVE VERB
When someone **frowns**, their eyebrows become drawn together, because they are annoyed, worried, or puzzled, or because they are concentrating.

grand ADJECTIVE
People who are **grand** think they are important or socially superior.

humorous ADJECTIVE
If someone or something is **humorous**, they are amusing, especially in a clever or witty way.

inn COUNTABLE NOUN
An **inn** is a small hotel or pub, usually an old one.

inquest COUNTABLE NOUN
When an **inquest** is held, a public official hears evidence about someone's death in order to find out the cause.

inspector COUNTABLE NOUN
In Britain, an **inspector** is an officer in the police who is higher in rank than a sergeant and lower in rank than a superintendent.

intuition VARIABLE NOUN
Your **intuition** are unexplained feelings you have that something is true even when you have no evidence or proof of it.

letterbox COUNTABLE NOUN
A **letterbox** is a rectangular hole in a door or a small box at the entrance to a building into which letters and small parcels are delivered.

loaded ADJECTIVE
When a weapon such as a gun is **loaded**, there is a bullet or missile in it so that it is ready to use.

lodge COUNTABLE NOUN
A **lodge** is a small house at the entrance to the grounds of a large house.

lodger COUNTABLE NOUN
A **lodger** is a person who pays money to live in someone else's house.

lord COUNTABLE NOUN
In Britain, a **lord** is a man who has a high rank in the nobility, for example an earl, a viscount, or a marquis.

lovingly ADVERB
If someone does something **lovingly**, they do it in a way that shows love to other people.

magistrate COUNTABLE NOUN
A **magistrate** is an official who acts as a judge in law courts which deal with minor crimes or disputes.

maid COUNTABLE NOUN
A **maid** is a woman who works as a servant in a hotel or private house.

Mauser® COUNTABLE NOUN
A **Mauser**® is a type of automatic pistol.

overhear TRANSITIVE VERB
If you **overhear** someone, you hear what they are saying when they are not talking to you and they do not know that you are listening.

overturn INTRANSITIVE VERB
If you **overturn** something, it turns upside down or on its side.

picric acid UNCOUNTABLE NOUN
Picric acid is a poisonous yellow acid.

pistol COUNTABLE NOUN
A **pistol** is a small gun.

poach INTRANSITIVE VERB
If someone **poaches**, they illegally catch fish, animals, or birds on someone else's property.

sermon COUNTABLE NOUN
A **sermon** is a talk on a religious or moral subject that is given by a member of the clergy as part of a church service.

silencer COUNTABLE NOUN
A **silencer** is a device that is fitted onto a gun to make it very quiet when it is fired.

stride INTRANSITIVE VERB
If you **stride** somewhere, you walk there with quick, long steps. The past tense of stride is 'strode'.

tazza COUNTABLE NOUN
A **tazza** is a shallow dish shaped like a saucer and either mounted on a foot, or on a stem and foot. Tazza is the Italian word for 'cup'.

trap COUNTABLE NOUN
A **trap** is a trick that is intended to catch or deceive someone.

unrecognizable ADJECTIVE
If someone or something is **unrecognizable**, they have become impossible to recognize or identify, for example because they have been greatly changed or damaged.

value TRANSITIVE VERB
When experts **value** something, they decide how much money it is worth.

verdict COUNTABLE NOUN
In a court of law, the **verdict** is the decision that is given by the jury or judge at the end of a trial.

vicar COUNTABLE NOUN
A **vicar** is an Anglican priest who is in charge of a church and the area it is in, which is called a parish.

vicarage COUNTABLE NOUN
A **vicarage** is a house in which a vicar lives.

watchful ADJECTIVE
Someone who is **watchful** notices everything that is happening.

wickedness UNCOUNTABLE NOUN
Wickedness is the quality of being very bad and deliberately harmful to people.

worship TRANSITIVE VERB
If you **worship** someone or something, you love them or admire them very much.

COLLINS ENGLISH READERS ONLINE

Go online to discover the following useful resources for teachers and students:

- Downloadable audio of the story

- Classroom activities, including a plot synopsis

- Student activities, suitable for class use or for self-studying learners

- A level checker to ensure you are reading at the correct level

- Information on the Collins COBUILD Grading Scheme

All this and more at **www.collinselt.com/readers**